Kyle
FiNDS HER
WAY

Susie Salom

Arthur A. Levine Books
An Imprint of Scholastic Inc.

Text copyright © 2016 by Susie Salom

Names: Salom, Susie, author.
Title: Kyle finds her way / Susie Salom.
Description: First edition. | New York, NY : Arthur A. Levine Books,
   an imprint of Scholastic Inc., 2016. | ©2016 | Summary: On her
   first day in sixth grade Kyle Constantini punches a bully who is
   bothering Marcy, a deaf classmate—and so begins her tumultuous
   year at Georgia O'Keeffe Middle School, in a different school than
   her twin brother, with new friends, new enemies, and the regional
   NAVS competition to come.
Identifiers: LCCN 2016008852| ISBN 9780545852661
   (hardcover : alk. paper) |
Subjects: LCSH: Middle schools—Juvenile fiction. | Twins—Juvenile
   fiction. | Brothers and sisters—Juvenile fiction. | Friendship—
   Juvenile fiction. | Deaf children—Juvenile fiction. | Bullies—
   Juvenile fiction. | Orienteering—Juvenile fiction. | CYAC: Middle
   schools—Fiction. | Schools—Fiction. | Twins—Fiction. | Brothers
   and sisters—Fiction. | Friendship—Fiction. | Deaf—Fiction. |
   People with disabilities—Fiction. | Bullying—Fiction. |
   Orienteering—Fiction.
Classification: LCC PZ7.1.S253 Ky 2016 | DDC 813.6—dc23
LC record available at http://lccn.loc.gov/2016008852

10 9 8 7 6 5 4 3 2 1   16 17 18 19 20

Printed in the U.S.A. 23

First edition, October 2016

for Belinda, my everything

and for Natalie, with thanks from my heart

Chapter One

Girl Houdini.

That's the name my older brother Roger gave me for my freaky ability to find my way out of crud-bomb situations like this one. But I mean, look at this place!

Georgia O'Keeffe Middle opens up like the beak of a giant octopus and my heart drops into my Vans as a wave of sixth and seventh graders squishes me through its man-eating doors. Wish I could shoot a harpoon to the ceiling and shimmy the rope to scout from on high for my best friends Sheroo Malagares and Brooke Jeblanco. Instead, I just stand there with my feet glued past the entrance like a couple of chunks of chignitrium.

Some Houdini.

"Constantini!"

(Hey, that rhymes.)

Sheroo and Brooke bubble up from the crowd like life

preservers and I barely stop myself from flinging my arms around their shoulders like a drowning woman.

"Heart attack *city*!" Sheroo screams. Sheroo's madly in love with screaming. "*Where* did you get your hat?"

I touch the front of my blue fedora. Not to act cool or anything. My fingers just sort of fly up there.

"Sasha Poblansky has a hat just like that today only hers is a *li*-ttle bit cooler since it has zebra stripes," Sheroo says. "I think I might want a hat like Sasha Poblansky's only mine will be, like, with a peacock design. Because I totally hate people who copy."

"Then you must hate everyone," Brooke tells her.

Sometimes it's like Brooke and Sheroo are from two totally different planets. Here it is, first day of school, and Sheroo's in swirly tights and a denim romper with a tiny rhinestone Pegasus on the pocket. Meantime, Brooke's busy being swallowed up by this enormous, dark-green army-coat thing. Not that it's bad. Brooke's always had her own way of making strange things kind of cool. Except for maybe that one time when her mom bought her these stripy pants that made her look like she'd been working on the railroad.

"There is *so* much potential at this school," Sheroo says all out of breath. "A ton of the guys from Rosa Parks and Aspen Heights." She stretches her neck to look down one of the halls. "He's gotta be here."

"Who's gotta be here?"

Sheroo looks at me and Brooke. "My first boyfriend."

Brooke sticks a finger down her throat and that, right there, is the moment I realize I'm somewhere in between. Not like I'm all, gimme a boyfriend or I'll evacuate to China! But I'm also not all, sick, boys are boba with a hair in it and make me need to hurl.

First bell rings and something hot blocks the entrance to my throat.

Panic, is that you?

"Quick," I say. "What homeroom are you guys?"

"6D," they both answer.

6D! *6D?* How on God's green earth can my two best friends since birth, practically, be assigned to *6D?*

"Which one are you in?" Brooke asks me while Sheroo checks out every guy that rushes by.

"Not 6D," I tell her. Then I try not to hate *6B* with all of my heart.

"Tough break"—Brooke claps my shoulder—"but see you at lunch." Then she nods at me and says, "Godspeed," which who even knows what that means. I watch the two of them kind of fast-walk to a classroom close by.

Why couldn't I have gotten 6D?

I stuff the paper with my locker combo in my back pocket and look around the huge, new middle school they built just like a year ago. It's super clean with about fifty jillion halls. One of them's gotta lead to 6B.

I grab the arm of the nearest kid as he hurries past.

"Hey, are you in sixth?"

He glances down one of the halls. "First year of secondary, yeah."

His voice is different. Like he comes from Australia.

"You're not from around here, are you?" I ask.

"Look, I'd love to have a proper chat but now's not the best time. I'm a bit late and so are you."

Is he English? I think he might be English.

"Okay, but are you in 6B?"

He nods. Relief!

"Great. Where is it?"

Second bell rings. Cuckoo for crappo puffs. We lift our eyes to the ceiling where the sound is coming from and he snags my elbow.

"C'mon, Fedora."

We squeeze past a group of bigger kids who look like they couldn't care less that they're gonna get a tardy. Then he leads us into a hall which has almost no one in it so we sprint neck and neck down the center. Our backpacks slap against our sides and our sneakers squeal against the Fruity Pebble tiles when all of a sudden he brakes. I slide a few feet past the door before stopping. He twists the knob and it gives — thank God — and we sneak into 6B homeroom.

There are only three seats left, all in totally different spots. He takes the one in the very back by the pencil sharpener which I never would have picked in a hundred thousand years. You always get pencil dust blown all over your desk and your hair that way. I pick the one in the middle, bobbing in a sea of faces I have never seen before in my life.

A tall lady in square pink spectacles that looks like she's from the sixties is at the head of the classroom.

I've never had a teacher with dreadlocks.

"Good morning, everyone. I'm Mrs. Arceneau."

She dives into taking roll and, for a second, all I can think is how do you make your hair into a dreadlock? But then I sneak a look around my new class and start to wonder which homeroom Chris Dixey is in.

I *kind* of had a tiny crush on Chris Dixey last year but not really. Well, I mean kind of. It's just that he had this freckle on his neck, right at the collar, and it would peek over his shirt when he stretched across the table in art to get a paper or something. Like it was saying hi to me.

Hellooooo, Kyle! I'm Chris Dixey's freckle and I looooove you.

"Constantini, Kyle."

"Here!"

"Diamond, Marcy."

The girl in front of me lifts her hand. She doesn't say, 'here.'

"Donahue, Donna."

"Yo." Donna's voice booms from the back of the class

and I pop a look over my shoulder. She's sitting next to English Boy with one of her legs *hanging over the desk*. Last year, Donna had long red hair that dangled to her waist in two perfect braids. Now, her hair's in a greasy bob and — are those combat boots??

"Miss Donahue, kindly place both feet on the ground," Mrs. A. says.

Donna lets her leg slump to the floor with a thunk and I gape at her for a few seconds. I'm not trying to be rude or anything but it's kinda hard not to stare. Donna has always been so ... pink. Now, she's all ... punk.

Her eyes meet mine and she does this nasty smirk. Can this *ser*iously be the same person who wore jeans with rainbows on the pockets and was super into dolphins? I sit up straight in my desk and face back to the front.

There's something on Marcy Diamond's desk. It looks like an electric snail. She lifts it and tucks it into her ear.

Marcy Diamond wears a hearing aid.

"All right, everyone," Mrs. A. says. "Today is the day you will take your first steps down an important new road. Middle school is very different from everything that's come before because in middle school—"

Someone cuts a presidential fart. I think for sure Mrs. A.'s gonna be the type who ignores it when people go all Grody McGrodersen on her but then she surprises me.

"Part of my job this year," she says, "is to ensure that

the skills we develop in this classroom go beyond throwing sound effects out the window."

"That wasn't a sound effect," someone says. "That was a smell effect."

A second fresh 'n' fruity rips through the aisles and everyone cracks up. Somewhere, a mother must be so proud.

"Mr. Nevarez," Mrs. A. says, "if you need to excuse yourself to use the facilities, now would be an excellent time."

A huge boy with squinty green eyes and brown hair that sticks straight up behind his ears says, "It's all gravy, miss. Think I'm done."

A crazy-loud horn explodes through the hallways and a bunch of us jump a kilometer.

Fire drill!

Mrs. A. tries to get everyone to keep their cool as she lines us up by the door but people are still shoving and pushing. Because maybe they're all thinking what I'm thinking. I mean, what are the chances of it *just* being a drill when we haven't even made it through homeroom on the very first day? We pile into the hall and I sniff the air for the smell of destruction but make out only enchiladas.

Marcy Diamond is standing next to me. I stare at her for like ten seconds and send a command at top brain volume.

LOOK AT ME, MARCY DIAMOND.

Most people don't know this but you really don't need

anything more than a powerful brain to talk in ESP. It's better if you're a twin—like me and my other brother, Meowsie—but non-twins can do it, too, if they just work it a little.

I only call my brother Michael 'Meowsie' when it's just me and him. Hardly anyone knows we're twins anymore because he's been a year behind me since first. That happens sometimes when you're twins born in July. As my class walks down *another* new hall to get outside, it feels weird knowing he's in a whole different building. I wonder if he can sense that I'm in a fire drill here at Georgia O'Keeffe while he's still snug as a pug back at ol' Dickinson Ele-ments.

Marcy Diamond turns to look at me. She looks at me and smiles! I knew it could work with normals! Even though twin ESP *is* around seven times stronger than regular. She slides her hair behind her shoulders and I try super hard not to see if she has electric snails in both ears but, of course, I end up checking.

She does.

I smile back but then can't think of anything to say. Except that I wonder what it would be like to turn down the volume on the whole world.

Once we're out on the blacktops where there's all this construction going on, Sheroo comes running over.

"Sheroo, you're gonna get busted." I glance at Mrs. A.

"Just shut up a minute and let me tell you what I found out!"

"Scuse me, Fedora." English Boy strolls past and stands behind us in line. Sheroo eyes him up and down like a 3 Musketeers before looking back at me.

"Guess who moved to Montana." She grabs both my hands. "Chris Dixey!"

My mouth opens and something inside my chest—my heart?—gets all pretzely.

"Chris—"

"Dixey!" Sheroo yells again. "*God*, remember how cute he was?"

I swallow and look at English Boy, whose nose is in a comic book.

"Chris Dixey." I screw up my face. "Was he the one with the—"

Freckle. The freckle of love, Kyle. Gone. For*e*ver.

"—dark-blue backpack?"

"I don't know what color his stupid *back*pack was," Sheroo says. "The point is he's moved"—she shakes my shoulders—"to freakin' Mon*ta*na! Like there isn't already a shortage of hotness at this school."

English Boy flicks his gaze at Sheroo. Then he actually rolls his eyes!

I'm glad she didn't notice.

"What do you have second period?" Sheroo leans in.

"Have to check my schedge. Why?"

She grins. "Wanna cut?"

"What?" I say. "No!"

"Why not? I'll cut with you."

"Sheroo, it's the first day!"

"Well, what are fire drills for? Think about it, we're in middle school now. Practically *high* school."

"We are not practically in high school," I tell her. "And besides, what does our grade have to do with it anyway?"

The bell that lets us know we can come back inside rings. That was the cheapest fire drill in the history of false alarms.

Sheroo holds me back as the rest of 6B starts to follow Mrs. A. English Boy shrugs past us to follow our class. The second he's out of earshot, Sheroo mutters, "There he is."

"There who is?"

"The one." She stares at English Boy's back then turns to point at me all suspish. "He called you Fedora. Do you know him or something?"

"No, I don't *know* him or something. He's just a guy in my class."

Sheroo studies him as he gets closer to the school.

"You're so stupid lucky," she tells me. "He's, like, so much better looking than any of the guys in 6D. And that accent. So, 'Hul-*loo*, I'm from *In*glund.' "

Sheroo's English accent is horrible. Sounds like she's getting ready to puke up a petrified meatball. I picture him rolling his eyes when she wasn't looking and all of a sudden feel a little protective of her.

"He is cute," I agree. "But are you sure he's the right guy for you? I mean, he might be a little *too* British."

She narrows her eyes. "What are you getting at?"

I look back to the entrance right as English Boy turns his head and makes lightning-fast eye contact with me. Which, btdubs, is the first step to doing ESP: establishing the connection.

"Nothing," I tell her. "Just erase what I said. We should get back to class."

She does this big huff.

"You're still a *to*tal baby," she tells me. "You know that? You're worse than Brooke. Maybe you should've been held back with Michael, after all."

I squeeze both fists at my sides. She knows darn well it bugs me when anyone picks on Meowsie. I mean, sure, everyone knows he's kind of quiet and dreamy but that doesn't mean he's not smart. Believe me, he's like the smartest person there is.

"He wasn't held *back*," I remind her. "It's always a choice which grade you'll be in when you're born in the summer and your parents make that decision. No one else. So why don't you go find Sasha Poblansky and her zebra stripes and ask her to cut class with you?"

"Well, maybe I wi—"

The last bell from the drill chops off the end of Sheroo's sentence. I turn my back to her before walking to the entrance where all of my class has already gone in. A blast of air conditioning slaps me in the face as I step through the doors and suck in a breath.

Crappuccino.

How do you get back to 6B, again?

Chapter Two

It looks like my entire homeroom has P.E. second period. Marcy Diamond, English Boy, Doublefart Nevarez and Donna Donahue are all in the gym as I go into the locker room to get changed. My school shorts and tee fit me kinda huge. I knew that they would, and even told Mom, but she said I'd grow into them in no time — that I was due for a spurt any minute. I look into one of the mirrors over the sinks and wait to see if this is the minute.

Chris Dixey is in Montana. I'm not even sure where Montana *is*. I don't remember half the state capitals from fifth-grade Social Studies with Mrs. Cromeans. I turn my head and do a Wallace Pineapple smile at my reflection. Wallace Pineapple is this character I made up last summer who's kind of a cheesecake but he thinks he's attractive. Bet it'd be rad to get turquoise tips. Or even just a streak in my bangs. Something really kick and to match my fedora instead of just boring licorice for hair.

Someone pushes open the door and I jump away from the mirror, hurrying out to meet the rest of my class that's already lined up on the gym floor. You're not supposed to step on it unless you're wearing sneakers but I've almost always got on sneakers. Blue checkerboard Vans.

"Morning, everyone," the gym teacher says. "I am Coach Yeung and this is your Physical Education class."

Coach Yeung has a welcoming face. His black hair hangs over his eyes and he shakes it back with a smile.

"This semester, we will be opening with a section on t'ai chi." He presses his palms together. "Who in this room has heard of the concept of *jìn*?"

As in rummy?

"Anyone?" He lets his hands float to his sides. "Okay, so, t'ai chi is an internal martial art, meaning we will be focusing a lot of our attention on *jìn*, or power. You will be learning about the house of your *own* power—its source and how it moves. And you will learn how to channel the power of your opponent and use it to your advantage. We're going to start the unit with something very basic called *tui shou*, or pushing hands. You will be paired up with a partner to begin your practice."

As he's matching people up, I cross my fingers behind my back that I won't be made partners with Donna. I really

14

don't want her pushing me. One of her forearms has a red-leather spiky cuff.

"Constantini?"

I swallow and raise the tips of my fingers.

"You'll be pushing hands with Youngblood." He nods at English Boy.

I picture him rolling his eyes at Sheroo and feel the inside of my cheeks go dry. This is gonna be humiliating. I can already feel it. Sometimes you can *smell* an embarrassing moment about to happen just like you can sense what they're going to serve in the cafeteria.

"Pushing hands helps you to feel your opponent's intention"—Coach punches his chest—"to understand the house of his or her power. Who here knows what it means to neutralize a force?"

Donna lifts a shy hand and, when she does that, it makes me think of the Donna I remember. Coach nods at her to answer.

"To make something harmless?" Donna says.

Coach smiles. "That's an insightful way to put it."

I slide my eyes to English Boy. He's looking straight at Coach. I don't have a clue where the house of his power is, much less how to neutralize it. Before today, I didn't even know *I* had a house of my power.

"Exploring the house of your partner's power helps

you develop deep awareness," Coach says, "almost like a sixth sense to help you see your partner's move before they even make it. But perhaps more importantly, it helps you to avoid exhausting your own."

"Exhausting your own what?" Doublefart asks.

"Your own power. *Jin*." Coach lifts a finger. "Allow me to demonstrate."

He tosses his clipboard on a mat as he and an assistant stand in front of each other. They reach out their hands to meet in the center. English Boy's eyes find mine and I crack the knuckle on my thumb.

"Chill out, Fedora," he says under his breath. "I know just as much about this pushing hands thing as you do."

"Yeah, but I don't know anything."

"Well, don't get all mardy mustard, sport." He smiles. "We're even."

I blink at the gap in his two front teeth. It's like three miles wide. I imagine myself sticking a finger through it but then wonder if, by the end of class, he'll be able to enter the house of my power and know I thought about doing that.

"There are two ways to raise your arm in preparation for engagement," Coach is saying as he and his assistant touch wrists. "You can use straight-line force or circular power. In *tui shou*, we will be learning how to use and master circular power with both the arms and legs."

"Pay attention, Fedora," English Boy says.

"*You* pay attention," I whisper back.

"I knew you were gonna say that."

"Did not."

"Did so. I used my sixth sense, is all. 'Coz I pay attention."

Coach and his assistant stop and stand still with their arms behind their backs.

"Now, I'd like to see you try it," he says. "I'll be going around to each pair to make sure you're getting it right."

Oh, great holy mackerel of the order of Saint Tuna Fish. Getting what right? What are we doing? How am I supposed to figure out my opponent's next move if I don't even know my first one?

"Right," English Boy says. "Constantini?"

I nod. "Kyle."

"I'm Reed."

He puts out his hand and I go to shake it but he curves his arm away in a circle and smiles with his gappy teeth. "Circular power."

I close my eyes and shake my head.

"C'mon, now," Reed says. "I'm only joking. Let's get this straight so we don't have to do it loads. He'll only give us more attention if we're not getting the hang of it, so just watch."

He nods at the two kids Coach is helping. I take a

quick breath. It's Marcy Diamond and Doublefart Nevarez. Doublefart will cream her! He's twice her size! Practically.

Reed and I watch as Coach guides Doublefart's wrist to gently make circles against Marcy's. Their hands look like kissing fish, swimming through the ocean between them. It's kind of beautiful. In a way. Who knew a kid like Doublefart could move so smooth?

Reed looks at me again.

"Right." He lifts his wrist. I glance one more time at Doublefart and Marcy then touch my wrist to Reed's.

"You're a happy fish," I tell my hand quietly.

"What?" Reed laughs.

English Boy is laughing at me.

"Nothing," I say. "Just push hands, already."

I concentrate on swishy tail moves as I make circles in the air with my wrist against his. His wrist slides down but, somehow, mine follows it.

My sixth sense! Some part of me *knew* his wrist was going to slip before it did. Girl Houdini: the Comeback Years!

"How'd you do that?" he asks.

"How do you think?" I grin. "Circular power."

"Please!" Marcy Diamond's sweet, yawny voice cuts through me and Reed's rhythm.

Doublefart has something in his hand. He's lifting it above Marcy's head.

One of her snails!

"Mr. Nevarez."

Coach Yeung is acting *way* too calm. Doublefart ignores him and does this devil laugh at Marcy, who looks like she might cry. Then he puts her electric snail behind his International House of Fartcakes like he's getting ready to use his one and only skill on it.

I can't believe my eyes. Is no one going to do something about this? I'm sure as schneck not gonna let some *dung buster* get away with torturing Marcy. I drop wrists with Reed and march straight over to Doublefart.

"Give it back to her, you blue baboon's butthole!"

Doublefart's eyes ooze in my direction. "What did you call me?"

"You heard me." I get up in his face. Well, in his neck anyway. "Now, give it back."

"You're dead meat, Wonder Woman."

"You leave Marcy Diamond alone," I growl.

I can sense Coach standing there, just out of the corner of my eye.

"Think you're Mrs. *Tough* Man," Doublefart tells me, "when you're nothing but a skinny baby. You oughta go to the special school for all the losers and wimpazoid little *ba*bies!"

Doublefart tosses something hard on the ground. I look to see if it's Marcy's electric snail and something inside me snaps like a cherry bomb about to go nuclear.

"Fedora!" Reed yells.

But it's too late. My knuckles have a brain of their own and they're already connecting with Jabba the Gut. For one second, I wonder if it'll be like Marshmallow Man—that my punch'll disappear into the rolls of skin blobbing around under Doublefart's uniform shirt and Coach will have to break into the house of his power just to get my hand back alive! Instead, my fist just bounces out and Doublefart smirks as the sound of a hundred breaths being sucked in fills the gym.

Coach's hand falls heavy on my shoulder as I slowly turn my head to look at him.

"Miss Constantini."

And that is how I get my personal invitation to meet the principal on my first day at Georgia O'Keeffe.

Chapter Three

Doublefart's real first name is Inocente.

As Reed would say, *right.*

Principal Bracamontes is curved and watchy, like a human question mark. He sits behind his desk half looking out the window, half listening to Ino—he says everybody calls him that—squeezing out his side of the story.

That's another thing. Turns out you're not allowed to call people butthole at Georgia O'Keeffe. Even if it does belong to a blue baboon.

"So, why did you"—Principal Brac looks at me—"feel the need to call Ino a name and"—he flips a paper on his desk to read it then looks back up—"punch him in the stomach?"

How can I get my principal to understand that Marcy makes me feel like Meowsie does? There's people in this world who are always taking it on the chin. (That's a saying my dad taught me: taking it on the chin. It means

21

getting served a crapberry tartlet and then not having any choice but to chow. He says he does it all the time at work.) To me, it seems like a lot of the times the people who take it on the chin don't deserve it. So, who's going to stand up for them? Who's gonna tell the people who give it on the chin to knock it off?

"Miss Constantini?" Principal Brac says.

"Kyle," I say. "My name is Kyle and—" I take a breath but then stop. I was gonna say I'm sorry I punched Ino in the gut but that wouldn't be the truth. I'da punched him more times if Reed hadn't pulled my arm back.

Principal Brac raises his eyebrows at me. "And?"

"And I think people shouldn't pick on people who are smaller than they are," I say.

"Well, what about people who are bigger than they are?"

"That was different." I lift a hand. "I didn't take something of Ino's to torture him. I just was telling him to give Marcy's snai—hearing aid back."

Principal Brac looks at Ino. "Why did you take Miss Diamond's hearing aid?"

Ino does this slurpy sniff.

Principal Brac takes a breath and then stands. He's skinnyish. Like a runner. Guess you have to keep in pretty good shape to stay ahead of the game as honcho of a sparkly new middle school.

"Inocente, Marcy has come to us from a special educational setting. She's been almost entirely deaf since she was five years old."

Five years old! Wow. I wonder why?

"She is a brave, dedicated student and she was chosen from her school to try out a new technology that will help her attend a regular middle school. Like ours. Can you understand how she must feel?"

Ino just sniffs some more. Ever heard of Kleenex, Monster Mash? It's this new invention.

"Miss Constantini—"

I straighten in my seat. "You can call me Kyle."

Principal Brac walks around to the front of his desk and sits on the edge of it, crossing his arms.

"Coach Yeung has been instructed how to handle these situations at a teachers' meeting. He doesn't require assistance from another student."

I stare at him and try not to blink.

"We're not all here to take justice into our own hands, Kyle," he says. "Do you understand what I mean by that?"

I blink. I couldn't help it. Eyes get pretty dry when you're in a principal's office.

"I'm sorry for losing my temper," I say. "But I also think Ino should apologize to Marcy."

Principal Brac taps his lips with a finger and looks at Ino.

"Inocente?"

"Sorry to Marcy," he mumbles.

"Not here," I tell him. "To her face."

Ino shoots muck out of his eyes. It's pignifying. I've never seen such a slimy stare in all my life and times.

"All right, Inocente," Principal Brac says. "You'll be on lunch duty for two weeks in the cafeteria. During recess, you can help the crew pick up the lunchroom."

"Aw, man! That's cheap!"

Principal Brac ignores him.

"And, Kyle?"

I look at him and gulp.

"I'd like you to pay a visit to Mrs. Arceneau after lunch."

"My homeroom teacher?"

He nods. "She's volunteered to coach our NAVS team this year. The event is in October and our team will compete against other middle schools in the city. The first meeting for interested students is today."

"Wait, I only have to do lunch cleanup for two weeks and she has to join a club until October?" Ino says.

Principal Brac looks at him.

"Gravy." Ino grins.

I take a second to think it over. Cleanup duty is the grossest thing on this planet and in this world. There've even been kids who puke and stuff. I don't know what

NAVS thingie is but it's gotta be better than getting captain of the barf patrol.

"Now, you can both take these"—Principal Brac signs two slips and tears them out of a tablet to give one to each of us—"and go straight to your third-period class."

Ino grabs his paper and peels out. I stand to take mine and look at it before lifting my eyes to my principal again.

"How come I didn't get lunch duty?"

Principal Brac rises from the desk and claps my shoulder.

"I'll be interested to see how you help your teammates tackle this year's challenge."

"Challenge?"

"NAVS presents the same problem to each participating school, and the team that comes up with the most creative solution wins. I hope you'll find the puzzle sparks your imagination." Then his whole face starts to change, like it's getting ready to smile. "Actually, I hope it engages your crusading spirit."

Soon as I leave the office, I go to the library to look up the capital of Montana and the word *crusading*.

Chris Dixey lives somewhere near the city of Helena now. And I have a spirit that is vigorous in defending causes and ideas.

Everything is so, so different this year.

After lunch, I find my way back to 6B homeroom by myself—progress!—and knock on Mrs. A.'s open door.

"Kyle, come in," she says.

Brooke! I didn't know she was a NAVSter! I wave at her as she slides her backpack off the top of the desk she's sitting in and gives me a quick nod. I wonder why she didn't tell me about this at lunch. Well, I guess it's fair since I wasn't too nuts about mentioning anything to her or Sheroo about my super chunkface adventures during gym.

Mrs. A. is sitting at the front, close to the windows, and Reed and another boy I don't recognize are in two desks next to Brooke.

"Welcome to this year's first NAVS meeting," Mrs. A. tells me. "I'm happy you've decided to join us."

I lick my lips then bite the bottom one. Wonder if ol' Brach Ness Monster bothered to tell her *why* I'm here. Then again, what difference does it make, really? The point is I've brought my crusading spirit to help the team win.

I take a seat between Brooke and Reed.

"Well, well, well," he says under his breath, "if it isn't the fighting Fedora."

I refuse to look at him. Thinks he's so clever with his gap in his teeth and his circular power.

"Come on in, Donna. We're just getting started."

Every neck turns toward Donna Donahue slouching in the open door. Her pants are saggy and black and her tee has two baby holes in the shoulder and says, TRY ME.

Brooke cuts her eyes in my direction and raises one eyebrow a little. I've always wanted to learn how to raise just one eyebrow a little. Whenever I try, my nostrils flare out and I end up looking like I'm hatching a plot to overthrow the emperor.

"How many of you are already familiar with NAVS?" Mrs. A. asks.

Donna flops into the desk behind Brooke as the boy I don't recognize raises his arm with a super straight hand. He's like a polite robot with very neatly parted hair.

"NAVS," he starts, "was my best part of last year. I've been competing with my old school since I was in second grade. Our team won two of the years and we had a pizza party with Panama Pete's all to ourselves before going to Regionals. Well, one year it was Panama Pete's. The other year I can't remember right now but I will in a minute. Sometimes I can't remember something right away but then all of a sudden it comes to me."

"Thank you, Cameron," Mrs. A. tells him. A little bit like, shut up already, Cameron—but in a nice, Patron-Saint-of-Listeners sort of way.

"My pleasure." Cameron nods. "What's this year's problem?"

Mrs. A. straightens a stack of papers against a desk then hands them out. I take one and read it to myself.

One of you begins in the center of a maze and cannot hear or see. It is the job of his or her teammates to guide this member from the center to the exit of the maze without touching him or her directly. Points will be deducted if the disadvantaged member touches the walls of the maze. Up to four team members can be on the floor at one time. You may not use anything that requires electricity or batteries. The maze will be the same for all teams and must be navigated in under twelve minutes. The judges will take creative costuming into consideration, but the most important criteria are innovative communication and teamwork. So, good luck! And may the most insightful and cooperative problem solvers win.

I stare at the page after I finish reading. You can't use sound. You can't use anything that needs electricity, and the person you're getting out of the maze can't see.

What in fire-roasted pig bottoms does this have to do with having a crusading spirit??

"I'll be the guy who can't hear or see," Cameron says.

Reed looks at him, then back at the paper in his hand. Donna tosses her paper onto the desk next to her and raises a boot over her own desk.

"Donna," Mrs. A. says.

Donna huffs and lets her foot slap to the floor.

"Where is the maze?" Reed asks.

"The mazes will be set up in an arena," Mrs. A. says, "on the ground level at the Civic Center."

The Civic Center. Huh. The sunken stage in the middle of that huge arena is pretty plush. I remember it from when I was eight and my parents took all of us to hear special guests of the symphony orchestra. These super-little kids, even littler than me, were playing violins like they were thirty years old. Afterward, the audience gave them a standing ovation. Must be nice to get those kinda props when you're not even in high school.

"You don't have to use every team member on the floor," Mrs. A. goes on. "It just depends on your solution. Only one of you will be blindfolded and wearing earplugs. The rest of you will be responsible for piloting your teammate from the center of the maze to the exit."

"Without using sight or sound," Donna says.

Mrs. A. nods. "And without directly touching him or her."

"This'll be a cinch." Donna lets out a bored breath. "The hard part will be explaining it to all you nerd bombs."

Well, ex*cuse* us for living, your maj.

"Right," Reed says. "And why, exactly, are you so sure this will be a cinch?"

Donna leans over her desk and looks straight at him. "Echolocation."

"You mean like bats?" Brooke asks.

Ooh, bats! I wonder if we could get stickers?

"I mean, like, dolphins," Donna tells Brooke. She shakes her head a little when she says 'like.' As if Brooke was a dorf pellet from the planet Butt Nog. Which she's not.

"You know, Donzie," I start, "I think you're going to have to be a little nicer to everybody. We are a team, after all. Even dolphins need another dolphin to bounce their sounds off of."

"Guys," Cameron says, "we can't use sound."

"Donna, why don't you tell us a bit about how echolocation is different in dolphins than in bats?" Mrs. A. says.

I really hope we can get stickers. I have a collection of funny stickers of bats. My favorite is an old video game one with puffy fangs and a cape that says, COUNT PACULA.

"Bats use air to carry sound waves," Donna says, "but dolphins use water. Plus, their brains are different. In some ways, more advanced than human brains." She rolls her eyes. "Which isn't saying much."

"Yes, but we can't use sound," Cameron says again. "Isn't anybody listening?"

Reed looks at Cameron and smiles, but just with his eyes. Reed's always laughing on the inside, it seems like.

"We can't use *audible* sound," Donna says. "Sonar has different properties."

"Yeah, but you can only use sonar underwater," Brooke says.

"Wait, you're getting too complicated," Cameron says. I'm glad he said it first.

"You wanna submerge the maze underwater?" he asks. "We can't submerge the maze underwater. Can we submerge the maze underwater? Mrs. Arceneau?"

Mrs. A. just looks at Cameron with one of her peace, love and brotherhood smiles.

"I told you the hardest part would be explaining things," Donna says.

"Try me," Reed tells her.

Donna's eyes fall to slits.

"Can't do it without a pool," she tells him. Then she looks at Mrs. A. "Can we have the next meeting at my house?"

"Of course," Cameron says, like he's the inventor of NAVS. "Some of the best brainstorming happens at people's houses."

"We're allowed to schedule problem-solving meetings wherever is convenient for all team members involved," Mrs. A. says. Then she looks at Cameron. "And I certainly appreciate your enthusiasm. It always helps to feel passionate about meeting the challenges ahead."

Especially if you get to have your showdown in a place with carpety walls and red velvet seats like the Civic Center. I think even presidents go there. Or at least a governor or two.

"The citywide competition will be held at the end of October," Mrs. A. says. "After which, the winning team will advance to Regionals in Phoenix, Arizona."

"Is there a Nationals?" I ask.

"There is," Mrs. A. says.

Kick.

"We can talk about that a little more as the time approaches."

"All right, next meeting's at Donna's," Reed says. "But for now, I have one more question."

"By all means." Mrs. A. looks at him.

"We can't use sight or sound," he says, "but can we use the sense of smell?"

"The rules say nothing about the senses of taste or smell," Mrs. A. reminds us.

Reed flips his paper over and scribbles something on the back with a stubby pencil. It's only the first day of school and already his pencil's half the size of a pinky.

"We're not gonna need the sense of *smell*," Donna tells him.

Okay, Mrs. Boss of the Universe. I mean, what's so bad about using a little per*fume* maybe? Some fresh-baked chocolate chip brownies or a lemon mint pie? (Sounds kinda good, actually.)

"The only thing we're not going to do," Mrs. A. says all calm, "is suppress anyone's ideas or contributions. Cameron, can you tell the rest of the team what NAVS stands for?"

He sits up even straighter in his desk—if that's possible.

"Negotiating Actions and Values for Solutions."

"Correct. And can anyone guess what that might mean?"

Crickets. Even ol' Grand Master Cam doesn't have the answer for this one.

"What do we use to decide how we are going to behave?" Mrs. A. asks. "Anyone?" She looks from one face to the next.

"Our values?" Brooke says in a tiny voice.

"Thank you, Brooke," Mrs. A. says. "And what does that mean, exactly?"

"It means"—Cameron stops and glances around—"how we act is a way to tell what we believe?"

"Precisely." Mrs. A. rests a hand on Cameron's shoulder and he gets this hotshot look on his face like he just solved world peace. "But it also means," she goes on, "that what we truly believe will eventually determine our choices."

"Can you give an example?" Reed says.

"I can." Mrs. A. nods. "Now, this is a really basic situation, but I think it might help. My husband likes to ski. I don't. *But* we both like to spend our weekends together.

So when he wants to hit the slopes, what do I do? Well, I ask myself what my values are. Number one, I value time with my husband. Number two, I value staying warm and comfortable. Number three, I value new experiences. So, instead of staying home when my husband goes to the mountains for the weekend, I go with him and find pleasant ways to pass the time while he's on the powder. I have used my values to shape my actions and find a solution. And that's what you will be doing as you work together as a team to beat this maze with the limitations the rules have placed on you. Make sense?"

Kind of. Only I'm not gonna worry so much about the details right this second since I think I'm the kind of girl who just picks things up as she goes. And anyway, who says Donna can't be right? I mean, what if this actually does turn out to be a cinch if we just, I don't know, use our sixth sense or whatever?

All in all, this is not too shabbs a punishment compared to Ino el Clean-o and his paradise of mystery meat. I lean back in my chair and put my feet up on the seat in front of me.

Thank youuuu, Count Bracula.

Chapter Four

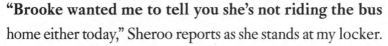

"Brooke wanted me to tell you she's not riding the bus home either today," Sheroo reports as she stands at my locker.

"How come?" I ask.

"She had to leave early to have some kind of tests run."

I slam my locker door shut and we move toward the front of the school.

"What kind of tests?"

"You'll have to ask her." Sheroo shrugs. "We still on for tonight?"

"7:07."

For years, Sheroo and I have had the tradition where one of us calls the other at 7:07. Not *every* single night or anything. But definitely on special nights, like the one after the first day of school.

"You call me or I call you?" she asks.

"How about I call you?"

"Okay, but don't forget."

I roll my eyes and shake my head. When have I ever forgotten?

Once we get outside, Sheroo crosses the front of the school to get to where her bus is waiting. Two buses from mine, I spot Marcy. I chew on my bottom lip. Wonder if I have time to go talk to her? I'd wanted to invite her to sit with Brooke and Sheroo and me at lunch, but didn't see her in the cafeteria. I start to walk toward her now.

"Fedora."

I turn to see Reed standing at the front of the line for our bus.

"Wouldn't take too long," he tells me. "Driver might leave without you."

I nod and he doesn't say anything else. Just squints one eye at me as I keep walking over to Marcy. Once I get to her bus, I stand there for a moment before she notices me. When she does, she smiles and I smile back.

"Is this your bus?" She speaks the words but she also kind of signs them.

"Is it yours?" I ask.

She nods.

"Thanks for earlier," she says. "You didn't have to punch anybody's guts out." She smiles a little. "Even though he was kind of begging for it."

I lift a shoulder. "Sometimes it's easier to stand up

for somebody you care about than it is to stand up for yourself."

She smiles again. "I bet you're the type who makes friends really quickly."

The sign for 'friends' is rad. I hook both pointer fingers together one way and then the other, just like she did, and we stand there and grin at each other.

The line starts to move. I don't wanna cut the convo short now that I'm actually getting the chance to talk to her. I glance back at Reed and rub at my nose with the back of my hand. I'm not sure how sharp his ESP skills are at this point, but I go ahead and give it the ol' Jedi try.

Use the force, Reed.

His eyebrows meet in the center.

Let go.

I lift a hand and hope he understands sometimes you just gotta seize the breeze. The big tree at the curb shakes a little in the flowerish wind and my legs climb onto Marcy Diamond's bus.

Marcy and I sit toward the middle, away from the rough kids in the very back and the kind of dweeby singing kids right behind the driver. For the first few minutes, I just twist my backpack straps in my hands and swallow a lot as I look out the window. I almost can't believe what

I just did. What kind of values made me pick that action? Is friendship a value, I wonder?

"What street do you live on?" she asks me.

"Oh, you know," I say and watch how she stares at my lips. "What street do you live on?"

"Tierra Santa."

I twist in my seat to face her. "Hey, did you know that means holy dirt?"

"Holy land, actually."

"Oh," I say. "Did you used to go to a school for only . . ." I stop and crack the knuckle on my thumb.

"Deaf people?"

I tip my head and she nods.

"But I can hear now." She pushes her hair back and shows me an ear with part of a snail poking out. "Because of these. They're the first ones I've tried that have worked without any problems, and they're really slender. I had six others before these."

"How come you still look at people's lips when they talk?"

"It helps." She shrugs as she pulls her hair back in front of her shoulder. "Most of the time now I can make out everything crystal clearly but I still like to listen with my eyes. I still listen with my fingers."

"With your *fingers*?"

She laughs. "Want me to show you?"

"Do it to it, Mountain Dew." I let her take my right hand and she presses it to the window.

"Perfect timing," she says as a yellow sports car with gonzo loud bass zooms by. "Did you feel it?"

"Well, I heard it," I say. Because I did.

"I did, too," she tells me. "But with my skin first."

The bus squeaks to the curb and she tells me this is where she gets off. Velocicraptor. I was hoping her stop was one of the last ones but it's one of the first.

"Guess I'll see you in the morning," she says.

"Yeah." I give her a big, phony smile to hide how nervous I all of a sudden am. "See ya."

Once she steps off, I look out the window at her front yard. It's pretty spotless. There's a sign in the front that says, ROOM FOR RENT, and I wonder if Marcy has brothers or sisters.

The bus pulls back onto the street and I notice I don't recognize any of the houses or even the street names. I wish with my entire body that I was sitting next to Brooke on my own bus instead of next to no one on a bus that isn't mine. Where is it gonna take me? And how will I ever get back to civilization after it does?

MAYDAY! MAYDAY!

KYLE TO MEOWSIE.

I'M GOING THROUGH THE DESERT ON A BUS WITH NO NAME!

As the strange houses whiz by, I try to think what I should tell the driver. Maybe I can just say I got on the green bus by mistake. That I've been color blind since I was five years old.

But then what if she gives me a lie detector and can tell I'm bustin' a whopps? And then what if she reports me! I'll be banned from all buses and Mom or Dad will have to pick me up from school every day—or worse. They might hire our neighbor Mrs. Ockfatrea to come get me and I'll have to hold in my puke or hurt her feelings and rock the nose plugs. (The back of her car smells like vegetables and armpit.)

Something outside the window at the next stop makes me melt in relief.

Meowsie.

He's waiting on the seat of his bicycle and in the basket of his bike is his old skateboard. The driver opens the door and I give her a quick look before running off with the kids from this stop. The bus does a loud crying noise as it pulls away from the curb and I grab Meowsie's shoulders.

"You," I say, "are the *sa*vior of the universe. Also, the champion of twin ESP."

He glances at one of my hands. "How was your first day?"

I let go and push up my bottom lip. "Pretty good. Made some new friends."

40

He drops the skateboard to the ground and puts one foot on it, passing me the handlebars of his bike. I get on and start pedaling down the street behind him. I don't bother to say anything about my special meeting with Bracamataco since I'm pretty sure I can get the discipline referral out of the mailbox before anybody even knows it's there.

"How 'bout yours?" I ask.

"I signed up for choir," he tells me. "There's this thing called Voices of the Future and my teacher said I should try out for it. That my spirit would become enlarged and I could hang it on a tree."

"That doesn't sound like Mrs. Marcus."

"It's a new guy," Meows says. "His name's Mr. Arriéta."

"I didn't think you were the type to be all, dude, just let me jam." I bang my head and lift both hands to make the sign for heavy metal. Then I stop before the bike tips over.

Meowsie shrugs, pushing with one foot to move forward. "I just like Mr. Arriéta. He says interesting things."

"Like?" I pedal slowly behind him, the tires moving in lazy half circles on the gravel and making a nice crunchish sound.

"Like that the universe is made of chords, not single notes. That every *thing* is actually an every *things*."

"I don't get it."

Meowsie brakes. His pupils seem to get bigger as his eyes move all over the ground in front of him. He does that when he's thinking of how to word whatever he wants to say next. Like when our cat Circe is playing lasers and getting ready to pounce—which is why I started calling him the Meowsmeister General in the first place.

"You know how there's a part of you that doesn't come to life until it's around a certain other person?" he says. "It's the part that's real not just because of you, but because of who you are when you're with them."

"Kind of," I fib. But then I figure, what the schneck? It's Meowsie. "Actually, I still don't get it."

"Like a joke, Kiki. Is a joke funny when there's no one around to laugh?"

I flare my nostrils, even though Meowsie says it makes me look imperious. (Whatever that means. I just like doing it sometimes.)

"And Mr. Arriéta taught you this stuff in music class?"

"He teaches Social Studies."

"Well, what does he look like?"

"Tall," Meows says. "He wears a goatee and doesn't look like a teacher."

He pops up the skateboard and sets it down before we take off again. I try to picture this Mr. Arriéta as we ride in silence for almost a block.

"So, guess what I found out today," I say.

Meowsie shrugs.

"That you can hear with your fingers. Oh! And sound travels differently through water. And people have a sixth sense that they can use during combat." I close one eye and slice a karate chop in front of me.

"Where'd you learn all that stuff?" he asks. "In class?"

"Most of it, no," I tell him. "Well, the sixth sense part I did. In gym. There's this kid named Reed and I used it to follow his wrist. We were pushing hands."

We get to the end of the street and hang a right. I recognize the junky blue truck in the yard down from our house. No one ever moves it. It just sits in the driveway with a twisty pink and orange lei drooping from the mirror, getting more and more rusted. I'll bet it gets bored and wishes someone would take it on a car chase after burglars. Or even just a date.

"Why'd you punch a kid in your class?"

I stop the bike and let both feet touch the ground. "I knew it!" I say. "I *knew* you could feel what was happening in my day."

"Actually, Mom's kind of freaking out at home."

My ears get hot.

"She called the school because you didn't get off the bus at your stop and they told her about the discipline referral."

Craptain America.

I do a gulp and look at our house. The light over the porch is on even though the sun hasn't set. I imagine Mom inside, walking back and forth in front of the kitchen island and wringing the liver out of a dish towel.

"When Mom started yelling on the phone to Dad, I went outside and figured I'd ride to your school. I asked some kids from your bus if they'd seen you. A guy with an English accent told me you'd gotten on the green bus."

"That's Reed."

"Why'd you get on the green bus?"

I take a breath and look at our front porch again.

"Meows, do you want to run away with me and live under a bridge?" I ask him.

"No."

We get to the edge of our yard and stop by the mailbox. It has the huge numbers of our address in those stickers that get all glittery at night when a car shines its lights on them. I pick at the curly edge of the 4. Meowsie nudges my arm and we put his bike and skateboard in the greenhouse off to the side of our driveway. There's no plants in there. Just tools and whatever.

"Just so you know," he tells me, "I'm pretty sure you're grounded."

I stare at the kitchen window.

"Why *did* you slug that guy, anyway?"

"'Cause he took a girl's hearing aid and he wouldn't

give it back." I turn to look at him. "He was bigger than her."

Meowsie thinks about this.

"There's a lot of dirt wads in this world, Kiki. Don't let them turn you into one of them."

"Okay, I won't." I look at the kitchen window again and lick my lips.

"Anger isn't about what you feel," he says. "It's about what you do when it comes. Same goes for fear."

"Okay, but will you please just stay with me when I go inside to see Mom?"

Meowsie scratches the side of his neck.

"Yeah, all right," he says. "But if she starts to scream too loud, I might go to my room. I don't like it when any-body starts to scream too loud."

"Yeah, me too," I say. Then I swallow and turn to face our front door.

Chapter
Five

6:59.

I stand by the door of my room straining to hear. I overheard Mom telling Dad that she was gonna go to the grocery store like fifty years ago but she's still sitting there in the kitchen, sipping on her matcha.

It's eight minutes until I have to call Sheroo and I'm not *exac*tly sure but I'm *pre*tty sure that I'm not allowed to use the phone. Mom already told me all I can do for two weeks is go to school and NAVS. That if my friends are doing anything fun after the meetings, I'm not allowed to stay. I need to leave once official business is over and come straight home to think about what I did.

Dad just gave me a pat on the back and a quick lecture on how violence is never the answer but Mom was ballistic. She said that, after punching a kid in my class, getting on the wrong bus was 'further evidence of a reckless mind.' I wanted to tell her, 'Oh, yeah? Well, what's reckless about a mind that can do ESP with a person they've never even talked to?' but I didn't bother.

Because the thing is, I wasn't trying to be reckless. Not when I stood up to Ino or when I got on the bus with Marcy. I just wish I could find the words to explain to Mom what makes me do things sometimes but then she gets so enormous in my face. And then all I can do is nod and say, 'Yes, ma'am,' when what I *really* feel like doing is turning into someone even more enormous so that my side of the story doesn't get drowned out by all the *kwa-kwa-mua-kwa-kwa-kwaaaaa*.

The front door opens and shuts.

7:03.

I slip into the kitchen where Mom's mug is sitting in the sink filled with soapy water. Dad's phone is charging so I quietly unplug it and steal into the hall to go to my room and shut the door.

7:06.

I start to dial Sheroo's number. It's on speakerphone so the first digit comes out loud enough to wake up the dead. I jump and try to figure out how to mute the stupid thing. Mom's phone is so much easier to navigate than Dad's. I accidentally press the camera on and when I try to turn it off, it reverses. I see my face on the screen and can't resist a little Wallace Pineapple grin. I snap the pic and notice the time.

7:08!

I quickly dial Sheroo's number and she picks up on the first ring.

"7:09!" she squeals. "Late! By two whole minutes! I've been sitting here *wai*ting and *waiii*ting."

"Sheroo, can you keep it down?" I whisper. Even though I'm pretty sure Dad can't hear her voice over the phone.

"Where are you?" she asks. "Are you in a library or something?"

"Why would I be in a library after seven o'clock at night?"

"I don't *know*! You're all whispery. And plus I thought you'd forgotten."

"When do I ever forget?" I say louder than I mean to. Then I lower my voice. "When do I ever forget?"

"Well, never mind about that," she says. "Did you know Sasha Poblansky is having a back-to-school party?"

I let out a long breath.

"Doesn't that sound great?" she shrieks.

"I guess."

"What do you mean, you guess? I bet she has the numbers of all the hottest guys. And they'll come if she invites them."

"Thought you said there was a shortage of hotness at our school."

"Roger?"

Holy Houdini. It's Dad! I can hear him calling my brother from down the hall. I freeze in the corner by the window with the phone to my ear.

Maybe he'll think I'm a lamp.

"There is a shortage," Sheroo is saying. "But it's not, like, a *fa*mine. I mean, there's that British guy," she says. Then her voice goes to mush. "Reed Youngblood."

A bolt of sugar zings through my guttal area when I hear his name.

Weird.

"Even if he's the only one Sasha invites, it'd be good enough for me," Sheroo finishes.

"Roger, have you seen my phone?"

Dad is *right* outside my door. My heart is wrapping its legs around my ribs like a spider.

"Sheroo, I have to go," I tell her. "And anyhow, I can't go to Sasha Poblansky's because I'm grounded."

"Grounded?"

I nod. Even though she can't see me. "Yes, and I'm not supposed to be on the phone but I snuck my dad's and he's asking Roger where it is."

There's a knock at my door. I shake my hands and drop Dad's phone. It goes skidding across the floor and thwacks against the closet.

"Kyle?"

"Why are you grounded?" I can hear Sheroo asking.

"Just a minute!" I yell at Dad. I pick up the phone. "Look, Sheroo, I really have to go! I'll tell you everything at school tomorrow."

"But you *do* agree Reed Youngblood is cute?" she asks. "Right?"

"Ky-yle!"

"Yes! He's just...smashing," I tell Sheroo. "I have to go. Bye!"

I cut the call and stuff Dad's phone under a sweater on my bed. Then I cross the room to my door.

"What's up?" I give Dad my best Bambi eyes.

"Kyle, have you seen my phone?"

"It's not charging in the kitchen?"

Notice I did not lie.

"I thought that's where I'd left it," Dad says. "But it's not there."

"Want me to help you look?"

"Sure," Dad says. "I guess. Michael!"

He starts to move down the hall.

I slump against the door frame and let out the longest breath in captivity. Soon as Dad goes to the den where Meowsie's doing homework, I grab his phone and tip-jog into him and Mom's room. Then I dump it in the pocket of one of his pants and sprint back down the hall, sliding in my socks past the entrance to my room before pulling myself in and slamming the door.

★ ★ ★

I wish Meows went to Georgia O'Keeffe. As I stand on the sidewalk waiting for my bus while he gets on his, I feel like my sadness will swallow me up. Or at the very least it'll lick me top to bottom like a thirsty camel. I don't want to go to 6B homeroom and I don't want to go to gym. I don't want to do anything but stay in my room and look at stickers of bats.

There's not that many kids in the seats when I get on the orange bus. Brooke's already sitting toward the middle with her curly hair floating around her face in a brown cloud. She's looking out the window and wearing a mysterious patch near the inside of her elbow.

I feel a shot of energy and move quickly to slide in next to her.

"What's with the patch?" I say. "And why didn't you tell me about the tests?"

"Tests?"

"Brooke."

"Heard you got grounded," she says.

I hate it when Brooke turns into a wall. It's like, c'mon already.

"Don't change the subject," I tell her. "And by the way, who told you? Lemme guess. Sheroo."

The corner of Brooke's mouth tugs up. God, Sheroo has a big mouth.

"Well, the two of you can go have the time of your life with ol' Zebra Stripes Poblansky because I'm not allowed to go. I'm officially grounded from all forms of life except school and NAVS."

"Relax," she says. "I'm not going to Sasha's party, either."

"Why not?"

Brooke shrugs.

"Because of the tests?"

"Can we just drop it about the tests?"

I lean into her face with one squinty eye until my lashes almost touch her cheek. "But you ad*mit* there were tests."

"So, did you get the book thrown at you?" Reed slides into the seat behind Brooke and me.

I can't tell if he just got on or if he was hanging around the back of the bus and moved up but all of a sudden, there he is—smacking his backpack against the window near his seat and hanging his arms over mine and Brooke's. I don't know what getting the book thrown at me means so I just lift a cool shoulder.

"She's not allowed to do anything but school and NAVS for two weeks," Brooke tells him.

"You've got a taste for trouble. Don't you, Fedora?"

"Ignore him," I tell Brooke. Then I imagine I'm a secret agent being asked a bunch of questions so I make a face like a cyborg and poke a hole in the seat in front of me with my electronic eyes.

"Hey, look, you should be thanking me," Reed says. "I'm the one who told your boyfriend where to find you."

"Your boyfriend?" Brooke makes a face. "What boyfriend? You have a boyfriend?"

"Stop saying boyfriend." I look at the ceiling. It's mega dirty and grey. Is that ketchup?

"Well, some guy was asking after you at my stop yesterday and I told him you'd gotten on the green bus."

"It was Michael," I tell Brooke.

"Why'd you get on the green bus?" she asks.

"Who's Michael?" Reed says.

I put my hands over both ears and sink into the seat. I'd make a terrible secret agent.

"Michael's her twin," Brooke says.

"You have a twin?" Reed asks.

"No, Michael's my Schwinn. I have a bicycle for a brother."

Reed smiles at me with his eyes and a fuzzy butterfly beats its wings against the back of my belly button.

"So, how come your brother doesn't go to our school?" he asks.

"Can we just talk about someone else's business?" I yell. "Or how about *no*body's! Just everyone be quiet."

"So-orry." Reed slumps next to his backpack and disappears into the seat behind us. But I can still hear him when he mutters, "Thought maybe he was Chris

Dixey back from Montana, come to rescue the fighting Fedora."

Brooke lifts an eyebrow at me and I hug my knees to my chest and bury my face in them. The day hasn't even started yet and already I wish this whole stupid week was done.

★ ★ ★

There's something peaceful about the sprinklers outside Mrs. A.'s 6B homeroom first thing in the morning. Summer is hanging on by a pinky toe and I bet they won't be watering the grass around the track once fall gets here. I can feel it, too. Right around the corner. You can always feel fall creeping up on you, even if you're not totally paying attention. It's that kind of season.

Right now, we're supposed to be filling out a sheet that asks like a jillion questions about what we think. Mrs. A. says not to worry if we aren't sure about some of the answers because people aren't made to be put in categories. She says the inventory is not supposed to give us answers as much as it is to help us ask better questions. Teachers love saying stuff like that. Next thing we know she'll be telling us Godspeed.

1. Whom do you admire?

Whom. Whooooom? Hmm. The first name that comes to my mind is Meowsie but maybe you're supposed to pick an adult or a famous person and Meowsie isn't any of those things. I start to wonder if Meows would put Mr. Arriéta on his paper and, out of nowhere, I picture Coach Yeung. He was so cool on the first day of P.E. but the thing is, somebody had to stick up for sweet ol' Marce. I mean, what *should* we open the house of our power for, if not to fight for our friends?

I skip the question.

2. Why do you admire this person?

Guess you're not allowed to skip.

3. What lights do you steer by? When faced with a choice, what do you use to help you decide?

Why do grown-ups ask questions like that? Who sits around thinking about steering? I mean, what am I, the merchant marines?

I blow my bangs against the tip of my fedora. I got it when Mom and Dad took Meowsie and Roger and me to an amusement park in Texas in the middle of summer. Some guy with tattoos all over his neck and huge wooden circles stretching out the holes in both his ears was selling hats at a stand. There were a lot of crazy ones with feathers and sequins and things, but I noticed my plain blue one right away. It was just sitting there, kind of not talking as loud as the other hats, but it did seem to whisper, *hello, there.* So I begged my dad to buy it and he said no. But after about twenty minutes, I wore him down.

I put down the first answer that comes to my head for question three.

I just point my fedora in the right direction.

Something tags me in the neck. I look at the floor and see a note folded up in the shape of a fish. Origami! I pick it up off the ground and turn it over to open it. It has three names at the top — Donna, Kyle and Reed. Two of them have check marks.

NAVS meeting at Donna's house Thursday!!
. Bring your bathing suit. <u>NOW OR NEVER!!!</u>
4412 Racing Court 4 O'CLOCK
~~Snacks will be provided but no dinner~~
Bring $3 for pizza Reed will buy drinks

Underneath the note is a pretty good drawing of a dolphin. I check my name and then write in my own message.

What about Brooke and Cameron?
I can tell Brooke at lunch
Does she have to check the note???
Also do we bring a towel

I hope we don't have to bring a towel because then Mom'll get all suspicious and think I'm trying to sneak in a swimming party. My bathing suit I can just wear under my clothes and she'll never know the difference.

I try folding the note back up in a fish but can't so I just roll it up and plan to tell the kid behind me to pass it all the way back to Donna. Then I think better of it and get up to sharpen my pencil. That way, I can hand it off to Reed. I wonder if they ever had races at Racing Court.

After homeroom, Donna meets me in the hall.

"I added Brooke and Cameron to the note." She gives it to me. "Have Brooke sign it at lunch then give it to Reed fourth period so he can get Cameron to sign it. If you don't have a towel, you can borrow one of mine."

I nod and watch her walk away. She's wearing all white today — baggy pants and a tee again — but on the skin above one elbow she's drawn a heart broken into lots of pieces with a red pen. She's a pretty good artist. I open up the note and look at the dolphin. It looks like it's smiling at me so I smile back.

I give Brooke the note when I see her at the lockers.

Hers is not super close to mine but I know just where it is so I make a point of getting it to her before second period. Marcy's not in gym, even though she was in homeroom, so I ask Coach if he knows where Marcy went.

"Marcy attends therapy on the last Tuesday morning of the month," he tells me.

"Really?" I ask. "What kind?"

"I wish I could tell you more about it, Kyle, but the truth is I don't know."

As Coach asks us all to line up, I think about how everybody gets to have all these extra things in their life. Marcy and her Tuesday-morning therapy and Brooke with her ultra-secret tests.

I suck in a quick breath. What if Brooke is getting tested for being a psychic? Maybe that's why she can't tell anybody. But if I've figured it out without her even saying anything, then maybe I should be tested for psychic, too?

"Your partners from yesterday will be your partners for the rest of the section on t'ai chi," Coach says. "I want you to get used to the way your partner thinks and moves. In actual competition, you would need to use what you have learned to anticipate the moves of a stranger, but for this class, I want to focus on developing your ability to sense what's coming from the partner you are getting to know."

I make a smart-person face like I get exactly what Coach is talking about. I want to understand more but, for now, I think the main thing that matters is that Reed is still my partner. Plus, I've already proved my sixth sense is working so I can probably just relax a little and use it during the confusing parts.

"There's a lot more to pushing hands than simply what you sense during combat," Coach is telling us. "Remember, it's just as much about getting in touch with the internal part of martial arts. There are thirteen movements in t'ai chi. By the end of the section, we will have tried to master all of them by first mastering ourselves."

The most basic movement, he says, is the one Reed thinks he's already so good at—circular power. It's weird because when you're using it, you're supposed to be messing with your opponent's center of gravity but at the same time be totally relaxed. Coach calls it the song.

I picture Doublefart coming after me and me just calmly whipping out my circular power. I'd be all *hwah!* and push hands and then he'd bow and be all, 'Wonder Woman, you *are* the master!' And then, of course, I'd be all merciful and tell him, 'Go in peace.'

"This warding-off movement," Coach is telling us, "is called *p'eng.* You will move forward and backward to both yield to and offset the force of your opponent."

"What do you mean, yield?" Ino asks.

"An excellent question." Coach smiles at him. "Imagine what it's like to punch water. How does it react?"

"You can't punch it," Ino says. "It just, you know, falls back or whatever. Then you're the idiot for thinking you can pick a fight with water."

Coach smiles even wider.

"Very good, Nevarez." He points at him. "Keep that. Okay! Less talking and more movement."

The assistant flicks on some music that's all violins and mandolins while Coach starts to go from pair to pair to help us with our technique.

"I'm bloody lost," Reed tells me under his breath. "Do you have any clue what he's going on about?"

I don't answer right away. I just stand with my arms at my sides, staring at the other kids in the class who are at least pre*ten*ding to know what they're doing. But after a few seconds, even the music starts to get on my nerves. I think it's supposed to get us in the mood to be ancient masters but about all it does is make me hungry for hot and sour soup.

"How are we doing here?" Coach walks up to me and Reed.

"Not so good," Reed says.

"That's a great answer, Youngblood," Coach says. "Admitting weakness is a solid way to start. Let's get you both in position."

Coach has us face each other and it's the first time I

notice Reed's eyes are blue. Not light like a glacier, or dark like the ocean in nighttime, but somewhere in between. More like the sky on a friendly, chirpy day.

"*P'eng* can be used to resist a push." Coach holds up a hand. "But note how the palm faces you, not your opponent. It is not an attack. But it *is* using the force of your opponent against them instead of summoning your own force."

"So you won't exhaust your power?" I ask.

"Exactly!" Coach says. "It is a way to resist aggression—the anger and fear of another—without giving in to your own."

Meowsie pops into my head and I remember what he told me yesterday. How anger is not just about what you feel but about what you do. Sounds like anger can also be about what you don't do.

"One of you will come in for the attack," Coach says, "and the other will use their arms to ward it off. Imagine making the figure eight with both arms."

"Is that why it's called circular power?" Reed asks.

"Look at you." Coach smiles. "The two of *you* should be teaching this class, not me."

Oh, go on.

After showing us how to stand a bit more, Coach moves on to the next pair. Reed and I glance at each other then fold our arms in front of us to start. I spread mine like wings to circle them when I spot Sheroo outside the door in the hall. She's mouthing something but I have no idea what she's trying to say. Reed looks over his shoulder and notices her, too.

"I think she needs to talk to you," Reed tells me as she slaps both hands on her legs and stomps. "Either that or she's having some sort of attack."

I glance at Coach and tell Reed, "Cover for me."

Then I sprint to the door and slide into the hall.

"What is the matter with you?" I say. "You look like—"

"What is the meaning of this?"

She lifts the note Donna told me to give to Brooke.

"Why do you have that?" I ask.

"You can't go to Sasha's party but you're having a secret party at Donna's with all your new friends and you invite Brooke but not me! You are *such* a *li*ar and a *sneak*!"

"Sheroo—"

"You can forget about sitting with me at lunch," she hisses. "Sit with Donna and whoever this Cameron is and"—she looks through the door of the gym and lowers her voice—"*Reed!* You knew I like him and you're purposely not inviting me because you want the chance to have him all to your*self*!"

"What are you talking about?"

"*He's just smashing,*" she says in a weird voice. "Just look

62

at you two! *Part*ners for gym. Why don't you just throw yourself into his arms and get it over with!"

"Sheroo!"

"You are a selfish friend, Constantini. And don't forget what comes around goes around!"

She tosses the note at my feet and turns on one heel, booking it out of the building in a galactic huff. I pick up Donna's note and try to stick it in my pocket but can't because I've got on my big, fat gym shorts and they have no pockets.

I walk back into P.E. on rubbery legs only to find Ino giving me a crummy grin.

"I'm telling," he says.

"There's nothing to tell," I answer, stopping myself before I call him Doublefart. Or worse.

"You're passing notes out of class," he says.

"Just leave me alone, Ino."

He flicks my fedora off my head and it sails to the ground.

"It ain't over between me and you," he tells me. "So, watch your back, Wonder Woman."

I stand there with my face getting hot until Coach says, "Stay with your partners."

I feel a nudge on my arm and turn to look at Reed. He's picked up my fedora and is holding it out to me.

"What are you, her little *bo*dyguard now?" Ino asks Reed.

"She said leave her alone, mate."

Ino steps up to Reed. He's about half a foot taller than Reed. Not to mention kinda, I don't know, meatier. Looking at him get in Reed's face, I almost can't believe I socked him.

Reed shakes the bangs out of his eyes. "This isn't what you want."

"Oh, and how do you know what I want, you little British monkey nut?"

I'm amazed Reed doesn't even squeeze his fists.

"What you want," Reed tells Ino, "is respect. And you're not gonna get it picking on girls half your size."

"Nevarez." Coach is standing next to us. He seriously comes out of nowhere. Like the Ghost of T'ai Chi Future. "It's imperative you remain with your partners."

"My partner ain't here today, Coach," Ino says. "My good friend *Reed* here was just helping me push hands." He grits his teeth at Reed when he says it.

"You're absolutely right," Coach tells Ino. "Miss Diamond isn't here today. My fault entirely. I'll need to set you up with a temporary partner. How about myself?"

Ino looks stunned. I think maybe he's never heard anyone tell him he's absolutely right before.

I know I haven't.

Ino steps away from Reed and me. "All gravy, Coach."

64

I stare at Coach as he leads Ino to the other side of the gym without so much as touching the edge of his shoulder.

"Don't let him bait you, Fedora." Reed swipes at his cheek with the back of his wrist. "Not worth it," he says. "I promise you, this sort of thing is never worth it."

I nod dumbly.

At the end of class, I sneak a peek into Coach's tiny office — squished between the boys' locker room and the girls' — on my way out. There's a cloth poster with a saying on it, pinned neatly and straightly to the middle of the back wall.

BE WATER, MY FRIEND.

At lunch, I'm sitting with Brooke and Marcy while Sheroo is laughing it up with Sasha and a couple other fuzz balls. (Okay, friends.) Sheroo's pretending to ignore me. I know she's faking because she keeps itching her shoulder with her chin so she can look back at our table. I want to go over and explain how the party at Donna's wasn't even my idea — that it's for NAVS — but Sasha kind of makes me feel like I'm not very cool. She's not super beautiful or anything but she does always have interesting clothes. And then everyone starts wearing something just because she did.

For example, today. Two of the girls at Sheroo and Sasha's table are wearing things with zebra stripes. Meantime, Sasha's in a sweatshirt that looks about as sturdy as toilet paper and is sliding off her shoulder. I'd be willing to bet that by the end of the week half those girls will be wearing see-through sweater tops that are three sizes too big.

Sasha's also got on earrings that hang down like pieces of chandelier and some shiny mint-green lip gloss. It's pretty but, man, I *hate* lip gloss. It always makes my hair stick to my mouth and then I end up spending half my life trying to spit it back out.

"Did you give the note to Reed?"

I turn to see Donna standing like a shadow over our table. I blink and pull the note from my pocket. "No, but you can if you want."

Reed is sitting by himself on a stack of red and navy gym mats by the corner, away from the crowd. He's munching on a nectarine and looking totally into his comic book.

"Well, I've already got Reed's check mark so maybe I'll just find Cameron myself," she says. "I'll pass out maps to my house tomorrow, but *don't* give them to anybody outside of NAVS."

She walks away before I can say anything back. I probably wouldn't have said what I was thinking anyway, which

66

is that I don't think anyone outside NAVS wants a map to her house but whatever.

"I think your friend might be a little mad at you," Marcy tells me.

I lift a shoulder and pull a banana out of my lunch sack. "Donna's always moody these days."

"I don't mean her," Marcy says. Then she looks past me and I know she must be talking about Sheroo.

I glance at Brooke who takes a surprisingly quiet bite of a carrot stick and raises one eyebrow. Curiosity starts to burn a hole in my brain so I turn a little in the bench to look. Sheroo's staring right at me as she whispers something in the ear of a girl I don't know. When she sees I've spotted them, she flips around to face away from our table and tosses her hair.

I swivel back to Marcy and Brooke only to find Cameron standing by our table.

"I look forward to working with both of you," he tells Brooke and me.

Then he backs away and walks off to where Reed is sitting. Reed's finished his nectarine and has the pit sticking halfway out his mouth. He doesn't move anything but his eyes when he notices Cameron. Cameron tells him something and Reed sets down his copy of *Wolverine* before offering his hand. Cameron glances at it before reaching his own hand out all funny — like he's afraid Reed's gonna take it and forget to give it back. Reed spits the pit out and tosses it by his comic book before hopping off the mats and taking Cameron's hand like they're gonna arm wrestle. Then he shows Cameron the three-strings-on-a-cup shake and fist bump, which Cameron picks up pretty quick, surprisingly.

Reed jerks his chin at Cameron and climbs back up on the mats. Cameron gives Reed a half smile then walks away, looking a little taller. Reed follows him with his eyes and smiles his laughing-on-the-inside smile and something deep inside my kidneys goes squish.

Because even though he doesn't have a freckle — just a gap in his teeth big enough to suck a fettuccine through — I think I might be starting to like Reed Youngblood a tiny bit better than Chris Dixey.

Chapter Six

"What do you think, Keith?"

Mom's slapping a nasty scoop of soybean casserole onto Dad's plate as I twist my hands beneath the table.

"It's for NAVS, Mom," I say. "I have to go because Principal Bracamontes said."

Mom gives me a look like I just socked *her* in the gut and Meowsie closes his eyes slowly and shakes his head.

I know.

Shouldn't have said anything about my visit to the principal's office. Chunkface move.

"Did you know they launched Pac-Man for the smartphone this year?" Dad says.

"Keith, put that thing away at the table," Mom says. "What kind of example are you giving the twins? Roger, get off the phone and come and eat your dinner!" she calls out to my older brother in the den. "Your food'll be colder than a dead man's tuchis!"

"That's charming, Nick." Dad spreads his hand over the touch screen like a magician and enlarges whatever he's looking at.

I wish I could do that in real lives. I'd make enormous pillows out of the ones on my bed and build a cloud mansion with those bridges that get pulled up to keep out all the gorgons. Either that or I'd blow up Dad's old electronic Simon and use it for the floor of a disco.

Mom moves around the table and snatches the tablet away. Dad flashes both palms and makes a face.

"Eat." Mom points at his plate. "And please help me decide whether or not to allow Kyle to go to the Donahues' house tomorrow afternoon. Circe, honey, for the hundredth time get *down* from there."

Mom lifts our cat, paws spread out like she's in the middle of a skydive, from the edge of Roger's place mat and sets her on the ground. Circe meows and bolts in the direction of her food bowl.

"I don't see what there is to decide," Dad says. "We told her she could go to the meetings. The principal says she has to go." He lifts a forkful to his mouth and makes another face. "Michael, pass your father the salt."

Meowsie tries to hand the shaker to Dad but Mom gets to it first.

Inter*cep*tion.

"You need to lower your sodium intake," Mom says. "We all do."

"Nicki, that is such outmoded thinking. Only iodized salt is bad for you. I deliberately bought the sea salt—"

"Roger!" Mom bellows. "Now!"

My older brother Roger breezes into the kitchen on his phone. He shakes his head and laughs into it.

"I'm tellin' you, baby girl, those pants were *ill*."

Off. The phone, Mom mouths.

Roger lifts a finger. He thinks he's big Kahuna 'cause he's good looking and in tenth.

Come to think of it, he is kind of popular.

"Yeah," he says. "No, no," then he laughs again. "Listen, I gotta go but I'll holler back at you before you can miss me. All right."

He slaps the screen and slides his phone into his back pocket.

"What're we having?"

My brother Roger is shaped like a model in a magazine—skinny with a perfect face. He's not very tall but he still has about fifteen girlfriends and everything they do, say and wear is crispy or ill. He's always gonna call all of them back before they can miss him. He must have an army of loverboy clones powered up in his closet.

His phone rings and he answers it.

"I'm listenin'."

71

Mom grabs it from him and dumps it along with Dad's tablet into the electronics drawer, then slides it shut with her hip.

"We are having," she says in a cotton-candy voice, "dinner."

Meowsie slips what he's reading under his leg on the chair. Me and him both still like to read books where you can turn actual pages so none of the stuff we sneak to the table ever gets tossed in the drawer.

Roger stretches his arms over his head and drops into his chair.

"Remind me that was Cree Mom hung up on," he tells Meows.

"Who were you talking to before?" Meows asks him.

Roger looks at the ceiling. "Sondrine."

I wonder if Meowsie wants lots of girlfriends like Roger. Do all boys want lots of girlfriends? I may have to bring it up sometime.

"Will your sponsor be attending the meeting at Donna's?" Mom asks me.

"What's a sponsor?"

"The teacher managing the team," Dad says. "Will he or she be there?"

I clamp down on my bottom lip. I have no idea if Mrs. A. will be there. Probably not. But maybe. I think probably she would be there.

"Yes," I say. "Of course."

"What are we talking about?" Roger tucks an entire roll into his cheek.

"Kyle is on the NAVS team at her school," Meowsie says. "She has a meeting tomorrow at somebody's house and Mom and Dad are deciding whether or not to let her go."

Roger swallows the roll after like three chews and shakes his bangs back, which out of nowhere makes me think of Reed. But then my brother does something I can't ever imagine Reed doing. He picks up a knife and looks at his face in it.

I wonder how many selfies Roger has on his phone.

"I don't see a problem with letting her go, Nick," Dad tells Mom.

"Keith, we have to enforce the terms of her punishment. We can't just be letting her out with her friends three days after she punched a child in her class and knowingly got on the wrong school bus. We have to nip this behavior in the bud." Mom snips the air with her fingers.

"You clocked somebody?" Roger looks at me for the first time.

"She was coming to someone's defense," Meowsie says. "Not just picking a random fight."

Roger looks from Meowsie back to me and smiles. "Somebody get this girl a cape."

"No," Mom puts in. "This is not something we want to encourage."

Dad moves his eyes to the salt shaker.

"Right, Keith?"

"Violence is never the answer."

"Exactly." Mom takes a seat and lays a napkin on her lap. She tastes a bite of the casserole and tries to hold back a gag.

"Needs salt," Dad says. "Tell me I'm wrong."

"I need a phone number for Donna's father," Mom tells me.

"What about her mom?" I ask.

Mom looks at me for a long time without saying anything. "What?"

"Honey," she starts. "Mrs. Donahue passed away in July."

"Was it the lymphoma?" Dad asks.

"It was," Mom says quietly. "Yes."

"That sucks," Roger mutters.

Dad takes a long breath and keeps his eyes on the far end of the table.

I look at Meowsie and he stares back without saying anything.

THERE ARE TERRIBLE THINGS IN THIS WORLD.

He gives me one slow, small nod.

Donna's house is different from how I remember it. I've only been there once—when we were all in fourth grade—for Donna's tenth birthday. It was a movie party and there was a huge blow-up Mario Brother to jump in so we didn't get to swim.

As I'm waiting on the doorstep with Dad, I'm wondering if there will be lots of pictures of Donna's mom in the house or if there will be none.

"Mom'll be by to pick you up," Dad says.

"I thought Roger was getting me."

"Roger wishes. He only has his provisional license. He's not going to be doing any shuttling around for another year," Dad tells me. "And even then," he adds under his breath.

I look back at the entrance as the knob starts to jiggle. Donna answers the door.

"You're the first one here," she tells me. "Hi, Mr. Constantini."

I say bye to Dad and step into Donna's dark house. The blinds are all shut and—even though it's hot and bright outside—the inside of her house is cool and quiet except for the air conditioner.

"What kind of pizza do you like?" she asks.

"All kinds, I guess. Except pepperoni."

"Who doesn't like pepperoni?"

"I don't," I tell her.

She rolls her eyes and lets out a breath. "Well, did you bring the three dollars?"

I pull three bills out of my pocket. They were flat and crispy when I put them in there. Now they're not. The doorbell rings and I have a chance to look around the front hall while she goes to answer it.

There's a framed picture of Mrs. Donahue on top of a table that has other things, like a big, pearly-pink seashell and a lamp. She's holding Donna — who still has long hair in it — and Donna and her mom are both smiling.

"Let's go to the kitchen," Donna says. Brooke and Cameron are both behind her.

"You have a nice foyer." Cameron waves at himself in a mirror hanging on the wall.

"Thanks," Donna mutters.

I glance at the inside of Brooke's arm. No patch but now there's kind of an orange stripe.

What sort of tests would leave an orange stripe, I wonder?

"Did you know foyers were originally invented as a place for people at concerts to get together and talk about the show?" Cameron faces Donna. "During intermission."

"That's fascinating, Cameron."

Donna leads us down the hall into one of those dens that's a step lower than the rest of the house. The room is really clean. Almost like no one lives here. Donna's an only child; this I remember. I wonder where her dad is.

"Donita." A woman in a Fozzie Bear sweatshirt with a thick black braid hanging down her back sticks her head out from the open kitchen bar to look at us in the den. "¿Quieren un platillo de fruta?"

"Anyone want fruit?" Donna asks.

"¡Sí, por favor!" Cameron perks up. "What kind do you have? I was hoping we would be having something other than pop and pizza. My mom says soda is pure battery acid in your system. We did an experiment once where we put one of my teeth that had fallen out into a cup of soda pop overnight. I don't believe in the tooth fairy so I didn't mind donating a part of my body to science."

Donna just stares at him.

"It was a quarter gone by morning," he finishes. "A *tooth*." He shakes his head. "You'd think enamel would be stronger than that but—"

"¿Tenemos sandía?" Donna asks the woman. "I hope you like watermelon," she tells Cameron. "Because that's all we're having besides pizza and battery acid."

"I like pizza," Cameron says. "It was originally invented in Naples."

Donna looks at him like he's an alien.

The woman in the kitchen brings out a large wooden bowl filled with juicy-looking chunks of red melon. My mouth waters. I didn't realize how hungry I was.

"I'll get plates." Donna goes into the kitchen. "You guys can sit at the table by the bookshelf," she calls over her shoulder.

The den is huge. On one wall, there's a glossy wooden bookcase, and right next to it are sliding doors that go out into the backyard where you can see the pool. Right by all the books, there's a table and the woman sets the bowl down in the middle of it.

The doorbell rings.

"Someone get that," Donna says from the kitchen, holding a stack of dishes.

Cameron and Brooke look at me.

"I'll do it," I offer.

I walk back down the hall and go straight to the front door, unlocking it before swinging it open.

"Donna has an answering service."

Reed smiles and my fingers get tiny bites of electricity at the tips. I almost feel like I want to jump a little higher than my skin will let me.

"She's in the kitchen getting stuff to serve the watermelon," I say.

He lifts two bottles of pop, one cherry and the other cream soda.

"Cameron won't drink those," I warn him. "He donated his teeth to science."

Reed and his older brother—I guess it's his older

brother because he looks just like Reed, only bigger—raise their eyebrows at each other.

"See you at half past six," his brother says. "And be ready, 'coz I'm not in any mood to deal with the old man alone tonight."

Reed nods.

"And don't drink too much of that." His brother looks at the pop in Reed's hands. "'Coz I'm not in any rage to deal with one of your little spacker episodes, either."

"All *right*." Reed tries to shove his brother away.

He skips down the steps toward a funny motorbike with a passenger bucket attached to it. He kick-starts it and buzzes away. We watch him sputter down Donna's street then turn to look at each other.

"You rode in that?" I ask.

"Yeah, I rode in it," Reed says. "What of?"

I lift a shoulder. "Nothing. Come in."

We walk down Donna's hall toward the den. After we each have a plate of watermelon, Donna leads us out the sliding door toward the pool.

"So, you're gonna show us what a *cinch* it'll be to suss the maze?" Reed asks her.

"Hold your horses," she tells him.

"Did you know that phrase was started after the invention of gunpowder?" Cameron says. "The Chinese had to hold their horses because of the noise."

"They don't now?" Reed asks.

Cameron looks stumped. But as we walk around the edge of the water he gets distracted by a little freestanding house.

"What's this?" Cameron peeks in the circular window. "It's got long wooden benches and black panels."

"You sit in there and sweat," Donna says. "It's for purifying the lymph. With infrared heat."

"Intriguing." Cameron nods.

"All right, everyone get in the water," Donna barks.

We take off our shorts and tees and stick the tips of our toes into the shallow end by the stairs. The water's not that cold but there is a little breeze swirling through the chinaberry tree in Donna's yard. It's already started to drop a few leaves into the pool. Once I shove my foot in to the ankle, it feels like the water will be warmer than standing around in just my swimsuit. I pull my foot out and take my watch off, tossing it on the lawn chair with my clothes and fedora. Then I walk to the deep end and dive straight in.

Underwater it's always super quiet. I let the air out of my lungs and sink to the bottom of the pool where everything is wavy and bright. The surface is kind of purple and smooth until a pair of legs surrounded by soapy-looking bubbles splashes in. It sounds like a hole being torn in the galaxy but it's just Cameron. He floats toward me with his hair all crazy on the sides of his head and waves with one hand. He's using the other one to hold his nose.

I push from the bottom of the pool and shoot up out of the water. Brooke has waded in through the shallow end and Donna is fishing out chinaberry leaves with a net. Reed is standing on the edge of the pool toward the deep end, staring at the waves.

"You getting in?" I ask him.

He doesn't say anything.

"You can swim." I tip my head to get water out of my ear. "Can't you?"

The way he looks at me — without smiling or saying anything — makes me wish I hadn't asked him that.

Cameron swims over to Brooke with just the top half of his head out of the water and splashes her.

"Cameron! You ever-loving pustule!" she shrieks and splashes back. Which only makes him splash her more.

I try not to stare at Reed as I wait for him to make some kind of move.

CAN YOU SWIM, ENGLISH BOY?

"Cowabunga!"

He crunches his whole body into a cannonball and splashes out half the pool on the way in. And that's all it takes. Cameron and Reed start splashing the Gorgonzola out of each other. Not just with their arms but with hard, thunking kicks.

I look at Donna through the spray and see her smiling. I didn't think her face could do that. She tosses the net

81

on the grass and does her own cannonball. She and Reed and Cameron get into this monster water fight but by this time Brooke's gotten out of the pool and has slipped into the hot tub. I take a deep breath and dive under the water, like a mermaid flipping her enormous tail, and see all these ripply legs and feet bouncing up and down at the middle of the pool. Cameron's trunks are orange and purple checkers and Donna's bathing suit is red with a picture of Emily the Strange. Reed's trunks are plain green.

I am a mythical sea creature, exploring this strange world of humans splashing each other for fun. My aqua tail swishes in a humongous circle around one pair of legs, then another. I stay under the surface until my lungs start to ache and cry and then I zoom up for air in a cone of silver. The humans don't notice the shimmering being that has come out of the water. They are the splashers. All they can do is splash, so I must join them. I must become one of them. I flip my tail and thunk at the first human. She is laughing and sending a huge wave with both arms at the second human who is wiping his face with one hand and splashing wimpily with the other.

The third human is holding on to the wall and making enormous splashes with both legs. This is the human I must conquer. I dive under and find a mysterious tube letting out warm water. It is my only weapon. My last stand. I shimmy toward the human at the wall and break the surface in front of him, drenching his face with the hose.

He screams like the little sister I never had and says, "Oh, you are really asking for it now, Fedora!" He tries to grab the hose from me to turn it on my face but I let it go and slice through the waves, faster than a hundred thousand dolphins, queen of the oceans of the entire planet and world!

I feel a hand grab my foot and try to pull me. My tail has begun to morph back into human form. I splash to the surface and see a tall, serious human standing in the sliding door to Donna's den.

"Kyle."

The human—otherwise known as my mom—looks really mad.

"Where is your sponsor?"

Sponsor?

Oh, Mrs. Arceneau.

Right.

I wipe my face and see Reed standing next to me in the shallow end. He shoves the hose underwater. Cameron and Donna have stopped splashing.

"I came by because your father forgot to ask what time I was supposed to pick you up," she says, "and you never gave me Mr. Donahue's number."

Her voice is calm but it's the angry kind of calm.

"Sorry," I say.

"Get out of the pool, please."

"Do I have to go ho—"

"Yes, I'm afraid you do," Mom says.

Game.

Over.

"Donna, please give my best to your father," Mom tells her. Then she looks at me. "Where's your towel?"

"I didn't bring a towel," I say. My knees are going to shake when I get out of the pool, I just know it.

"Why not? Didn't you know you were going to be swimming?"

I don't say anything. People have the right to remain silent.

Donna hops out of the water and opens a huge basket by the lawn chairs. She gets a towel for herself and one for me. I get out of the pool and thank her for it.

Mom just gives me that white look where her lips might any second disappear.

"Bye," I tell Donna.

She lifts her hand.

I don't turn around to look at Brooke or Cameron or Reed. I'll die first. Shrivel up like a raisin on the cool grass and just lie there until a bird gets me in his beak and flies away to his cave to eat me.

I pick up my clothes and hat and slide my sneakers on over my wet feet, following Mom into the house.

"I'm extremely disappointed in you, Kyle Alexandra."

World of Minecrap. Not the middle name.

I punch down my dread as Mom's heels click through the hall. I follow her past the picture of Donna's mom holding Donna.

"You have started off your sixth-grade year in alarmingly bad form."

We walk out the door and she snaps it shut behind her, taking the steps to her car. My whole body is shivering. She opens the door to the passenger seat and looks me full in the face.

"You're picking fights, making unsafe choices and now you're lying to me about the only thing your father and I have allowed you to do. I thought we covered this the other night!"

"Mom, I didn't—"

"I don't want to hear it," she says. "You have nothing to say that could possibly redeem this behavior. Now, get in."

I climb into the car and fold Donna's towel over the seat before I sit on it. Mom steps in on the driver's side and slides on her sunglasses.

"I'm going to have a talk with Principal Bracamontes about a more suitable form of discipline."

"Mom—"

"I said I don't want to hear it, Kyle." She starts the car. "You have shown me today that you are simply not to be trusted."

Chapter Seven

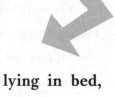

There are elves on my ceiling. I'm lying in bed, staring at the plaster, and can see them dancing around a pot on the fire. They are laughing and singing and having fun.

But not me.

I am grounded for an extra two weeks and — even though Dad says Mom is overreacting — I'm not allowed to stay on NAVS. Just when it was starting to get good.

I look at the clock on my desk. It's way past 7:07. Not that I could call Sheroo, anyway, but I do consider typing her a message on Instant. We don't usually communicate like that. We're much more better with words shared out loud.

I'm all twisted inside. Like if I can't fix things with Mom and NAVS right away, then I at least want things to be back to normal with one of my best friends.

I hear a bubble pop on my laptop and push down my

covers with one finger, thinking things must be okay with Sheroo, after all, if she's reading my mind like that!

But it isn't Sheroo.

It's an avatar with very long claws.

I throw off my covers and tiptoe to the computer.

Logan: so now did you get the book thrown at you?

Logan? Who in hairless hedgehog hineys is Logan?

the_amazing_kyle: I don't even understand what that means

I type it before I have a chance to think how dumb I sound.

Logan: it means are you in major trouble

I sit there with my fingers over the keyboard, watching the cursor blink. Ah, the schneck with it. Might as well just ask.

the_amazing_kyle: who's Logan??

I send the question then chew on my bottom lip, waiting for like fifty billion seconds before the answer comes.

Logan: it's Reed Fedora. Brooke signed you up for NAVS chats

My spine lights up like a Tilt-A-Whirl at sunset. Then I look out the window of my bedroom, wondering how many helpless hearts are out in the world.

the_amazing_kyle: my mom says no more NAVS

The screen goes quiet for so long, I wonder if Reed logged off. But his avatar isn't in sleep mode. Now that he's invited me to chat, that little cartoon guy with the super-long claws will hang out at the bottom of my screen next to Brooke, Sheroo and Meowsie's avatars until I delete him. If I delete him.

Logan: where's the fighting Fedora I know?

I roll my eyes.

the_amazing_kyle: grounded
Logan: aw come on you gonna let a little groundation keep you from the NAVS challenge
the_amazing_kyle: not like I can help it
Logan: sure you can. you know what to use
the_amazing_kyle: ??

Logan: circular power ☺

the_amazing_kyle: Reed what are you talking about??

Logan: Mumsy's upset because you were having fun at a NAVS meeting right?

the_amazing_kyle: she says I lied to her

Logan: well did you

I suck on my bottom lip.

the_amazing_kyle: kinda??

Logan: then say your sorry. tell her you didn't know ms. a would be a no show

the_amazing_kyle: Reed she wouldn't even let me talk at the table tonight

Logan: tell her the team won't be as strong without u

the_amazing_kyle: what about Donna Dolphin???

Logan: Donna Dolphin doesn't know sweet fanny adams. She just knows bottle nose dolphins use clicks to swim through muddy waters how does that help???

I take a deep breath and hold it until my cheeks puff out.

Logan: the team needs you Fedora

I let the breath out. I got assigned to do NAVS because I stuck up for Marcy. Now that I actually *want* to be in

NAVS, I could get into even worse trouble for staying. Seriously, what is up with the universe?

the_amazing_kyle: well how in the world do I change my mom's mind????

Logan: I know you Fedora

I blink into the blue light of the screen as my heart does a hop through an invisible hoop.

Logan: you'll find a way

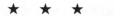

After school the next day, I go straight to the homework table and spread out my books and papers to look like I'm working extra hard. I want Mom to catch me slaving over my school stuff when she gets home from work.

"You wanna leave room for me?" Meowsie asks.

I pull some of the papers toward me and slip one of the books into my backpack. I don't actually have homework on state capitals. That was just an extra book I checked out of the library so I could have a bigger stack. Wish I had glasses. I could be super smart girl who has all the answers with my fat stack of books and my baby blue, super smart girl glasses. Ask me anything, I'd say.

"Meows, can I ask you something?"

He drops his backpack on the chair. It smells like orange rind and playground and has a picture of Yoda that says, THERE IS NO TRY.

"Shoot."

"Does every guy want a ton of girlfriends like Roger?"

The doorbell rings and he looks at me. "You expecting anyone?"

"Meows"—I lift a hand—"I'm grounded."

He gets up and crosses the den to answer the front door.

"It's for you!" he calls.

I get up right away and do a little run across the den.

"Marcy!" I say. "Come in."

"I got your address from the directories they passed out today." She takes one shy step into our house and Meowsie shuts the door behind her. She looks at him super quick and kinda smiles. "I wondered why you weren't on our bus anymore."

"How'd you get here?"

"Our new boarder dropped me off while she goes to pick up a prescription at the pharmacy. Just for like twenty minutes. I hope it's okay?"

"Of course." I swing my arm to the den to show her that my casa is her casa. "Marcy, this is my brother Michael. Michael"—I motion to her—"Marcy Diamond."

Meowsie gets a reddish splotch on his neck.

Marcy offers him her hand but he just blinks at it as the splotch crawls up his cheeks. I elbow him in the ribs and he moves his hand to shake hers.

"Come in," he mumbles. Then he sticks his hands in his pockets and backs away like Circe when we're getting ready to open a new trash bag. I think maybe the noise freaks her out. I swear, Meowsie's exactly like her sometimes.

"So this is my pad," I tell Marcy. "You want a homework snack? We have like a hundred oranges. Michael's madly in love with oranges."

Meowsie widens his eyes at me.

WHAT? IT'S THE TRUTH.

But then Marcy smiles at him again and he sort of smiles back.

"You still grounded?" Marcy asks me.

"Practically for eternity." I grab three oranges and toss one to my brother.

We move to the homework table and I clear off all my crud and dump it to the floor. Marcy looks like she's in pain.

"What's the matter?" I ask her. "Do you feel all right?"

"It's just—" She stops to take a seat and starts to pick at the orange. "It's just that you never would have been grounded if it wasn't for me," she says. Then she gets really quiet and I can barely hear what she says next. "And it turns out it's not even worth it since it feels like things aren't really working out at Georgia O'Keeffe."

"What do you mean?" Meowsie finally says something helpful.

"What things aren't working out?" I ask.

Marcy's face gets all pink. "It's just that sometimes it feels like it's all too much. Like maybe there's a reason why I was where I was before."

"You mean before you came to Georgia O'Keeffe?" I ask.

"Yeah. Just, before I transferred. Before we found hearing aids that worked this well and stayed working." She takes a breath. "Don't get me wrong. I mean, there's things that I really like about the way everything is now but sometimes, I don't know. Sometimes I just wish that my life could be the way it was. Less complicated. With teachers that I've known forever and friends who just *got* everything without me having to explain."

"I think I understand," I say.

"You do?" Marcy asks.

"Sure."

Meowsie stares at me.

"I think finding a way to make someone understand you is probably the hardest thing on the planet," I tell her. "Especially when everything is different. It's easy to feel like things are nutso butso at first."

"Even more so when mean people stand in your way," Meowsie says.

Marcy and Meowsie look at each other out of the corner of their eyes.

"Are you scared of Ino?" I ask her.

"No, it's not that."

"'Cause I'll kick his Hulky beehonks for you."

"Kiki."

"I'm just kidding," I tell Meowsie. Which is mostly true.

He takes a breath and starts to do that growing pupil thing he does when he's thinking. Marcy gets quiet as she waits for him to talk again. It's funny because most people kind of lose track of Meowsie when he starts to think before he talks again. Like they forget that he's there because he's kind of gone inside himself. But Marcy's not like that. She's more patient or something.

"Don't feel bad about Kyle being grounded," he tells her. "She's in trouble for more than just punching the dirt bucket who was bugging you."

"You are?" Marcy asks.

I start to peel my orange and shrug. "Kinda."

"She also got in trouble for getting on the wrong bus."

"My bus?"

"Sorta."

"Why'd you get on the wrong bus?"

"What can I say?" I pop in an orange slice and forget not to talk with my mouth full. "Guess I'm just a very adventuresome person." I give them a wink and one of those little clicks where you suck the side of your tongue with your teeth. I saw a girl do it on TV the other day and I've been wanting to try it out for a trademark.

"You have the spirit of a Polynesian wayfinder," Meowsie tells me.

"What's a wayfinder?" Marcy asks him.

"We're learning about them in Mr. Arriéta's class."

"Mr. Arriéta? What school do you go to?"

Meowsie shifts in his chair and clears his throat.

"He goes to Emily Dickinson," I tell her.

"Oh," Marcy says. "What grade are you in?"

"Fifth," Meowsie mumbles. "Anyway, Mr. Arriéta says wayfinders are a very rare breed because they don't depend on GPS or anything like it. They memorize the houses of the stars, where they come out and go back into the ocean, to make maps in their heads. They also use the movements of waves, planets, birds and sea creatures to set their course. Did you know that clouds get a brown color on the bottom when they're over land? If wayfinders notice the shift in the color of the clouds on the horizon, they can use that to tell them something about what's up ahead."

I feel a wave of respect for my brother, moving from me to him and then curling back. Just picturing the crud-face dorf nuggets who've picked on him for being quiet and keeping to himself over the years makes me wanna thump my chest and let out a couple Tarzan yells.

"There was this girl in one of my therapy groups," Marcy tells Meowsie. "She was born blind and she used to click her tongue to make maps of the rooms in her house with the echoes. Not every human can do that, but she could."

"So, do you feel like being in a school where you depend mostly on hearing aids is taking something away from you?" Meowsie asks her.

"No," she starts, "because if that's all that you knew, you'd think I wasn't grateful. And I am. But"—she looks at her hands and twists them—"sometimes I do take my hearing aids out. It's not that I don't want to hear." She looks back up at us. "It's just that since I didn't have ones that worked consistently for so long, I figured out other ways of being in the world. So when the hearing aids go in and I can hear everything in the normal way"—she hangs air quotes when she says 'normal'—"it's like the volume goes down on other mysteries."

"What kind of mysteries?" Meowsie moves in closer to Marcy.

"I don't know how to explain it exactly," she says. "But it's like, have you ever been sitting on the bleachers and you just knew someone was behind you? You couldn't hear them or anything, but you still knew they were there."

"How did you know they were behind you if you couldn't hear them or see them?" I ask.

"Because," Marcy says, "you can feel them."

"You mean like with your thoughts?" I get up on my knees in the chair. Sometimes when I get excited about something I have to move around a little.

"Not with your thoughts," she says. "I mean like with whatever part of you is touching the bleachers."

I scrunch my face. "Your butt?"

She smiles and Meowsie does, too.

"Ask the Great and Powerful Gazanka." I raise both hands. "It knows all."

Meowsie elbows me and I drop my arms.

"It's like," Marcy says, "when someone is standing on the bleachers behind you, even if they're trying to be sneaky, you can feel their approach depending on what you're both touching at the same time."

"Kind of like the waves in the ocean," Meowsie says.

The front door opens and Mom walks in, flinging her suit jacket on the coat tree in the front hall.

"Kyle?" she says in a tired voice. "Michael?"

"Over here," Meowsie says.

Mom comes around the corner and looks at Marcy with kind of surprised eyes.

"Well, hello there," she says.

Marcy stands and offers Mom her hand. "I'm Marcy," she says. "I was close by and just came to see Kyle for a few minutes."

Mom gives me an icicle look.

"You have a very kind daughter, Mrs. Constantini," Marcy says. "She's really helped make things easier for me in a new school."

Mom's face changes a bit.

"I was really scared on the first day, but Kyle was like my angel sent from heaven."

Now, Mom gives her a look like that's hard to believe.

There's a knock on the door. Mom moves back across the den to open it and a tall, blond girl with teeth in the shape of Chiclets steps inside.

"You ready, Marce?" she says after saying hello to Mom.

"Just a minute." Marcy slides a piece of paper off the homework table. "May I?"

"What's mine is yours," I tell her.

She rips it in half and writes something on it then hands it to Meowsie.

"This is my screen name on Instant," she says.

I try to look over her shoulder. I wanna know her screen name on Instant.

"I'd really like to hear more about wayfinders if you learn any more interesting things in your class," she tells Meowsie.

He takes the paper and stares at it like it's the map to El Dorado.

Marcy bounces across the den then turns at the door and looks at me. "See you tomorrow."

Then she tells Mom nice to meet her and says bye. As soon as she and the blond girl are gone, I plop open a book on the table while Mom stares at the closed door.

"Just doing *home*work," I sing.

"Is that the girl you stood up for in gym?" Mom asks me.

I stop flipping through the pages and look up at her.

"Is it?" she asks.

I nod.

"I just came from Principal Bracamontes' office." She steps across the den and comes to the table. "We still haven't come up with a suitable substitute form of discipline. All he offered was detention for a month, but I think that will interfere with establishing a proper homework routine. Besides that, Roger's not an experienced enough driver to be picking you up forty-five minutes later than the bus. I certainly can't be doing that for four weeks."

I picture Mrs. Ockfatrea waiting for me at the curb after school in her turdy Datsun and kneel in front of my mother.

"Mom, *please* just let me do NAVS." I clasp my hands. "Michael says I have the spirit of a wayfinder and Marcy's teaching me all about the ears in my butt and I can use all that to help my school win the challenge. I'm so sorry that I didn't know Mrs. A. wasn't going to be at Donna's, but I didn't start the water fight, it was Cameron—"

"Get up off the floor, Kyle."

"Yes, ma'am."

"Finish your homework and then come into the kitchen to set the dinner table."

I nod and take a seat, sitting with my back so straight my head might fall behind me. I stack a single loose paper like a secretary and search my backpack for a sharpened pencil. It's only the first week of school and already I'm out of pencils. There's gotta be a star map somewhere to lead humanity to the stash of missing pencils.

"I don't want you getting excited about this NAVS competition, Kyle," Mom says from the kitchen after she washes her hands and pulls a salad bowl out of the cabinet. "There's no way your father and I will allow you to go over to a team member's house while you're still grounded."

"Mom, Marcy's having a hard time at our school," I say.

Mom pulls a bottle of salad dressing out of the fridge. "I can imagine."

"It's hard for her, Mom. She misses her old school and she needs something to make her feel like this is all worth it." A flash of brilliance lights up my brain. "Like joining NAVS!"

Mom moves her eyes to mine. "I fail to see the connection, Kyle."

"We see what we wanna see, Mom."

"Don't sass me, Kyle Alexandra."

"Sorry," I say. Even though I'm not, really.

"It doesn't seem like grounding Kyle from NAVS is the only way to handle what happened at Donna's," Meowsie offers. "It seems like NAVS is good for her. And could be good for Marcy."

"That's enough from the both of you," Mom says. "Now, Kyle, Marcy is not your responsibility. If she wants to join NAVS, that is her business. I'm concerned with your business. The business of making sure that you are not acting out in a violent way, disregarding rules and then lying to cover up your actions."

Put like that, I do sound like a nerf herder.

"I'm sure that makes sense to the two of you. You're both very bright and I don't think I need to keep spelling this out."

"But, Mom —"

"No buts."

Yeah, right.

"Now go wash your hands and set the table. And what are all those papers and books on the ground?"

I look at the stuff I chucked on the carpet when Marcy came in and snarl. So much for impressing my mother with homework.

But hang on just a tiny second. Didn't she say that I can't be going over to people's houses? Because if that's the case, she never said a *word* about what I do with my free time while I'm at school now, did she?

Chapter Eight

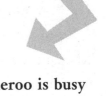

Monday morning before classes start, Sheroo is busy whispering and giggling with one of her new friends in the quadrangle. I don't think they're talking about me or anything, but I am a little surprised at how quickly she's gotten in with a different group.

Okay, this is stupid. I'm just going to walk over there and straighten all this out. Sheroo, me and Brooke have been best friends since the second grade. How hard can it be to just march right over and set the old record straight once and for all?

I grip my books to my chest as I try to get up the guts to interrupt Sheroo and some girl who—just as I predicted!—is wearing aquamarine lip gloss and a shirt sliding off her shoulder.

That's when I notice Sheroo is pretty much still doing her own thing. She's got on one of her corduroy rompers with candy-apple tights. I feel weirdly proud of her for not running out and turning into a creature from Sasha Poblansky Island.

"I'm going to the library."

Brooke is standing next to me.

"What for?" I turn to look at her.

"I want to use the computer lab. Send a quick email."

I shoot a last look at Sheroo and her new friend as they move into the bathroom, away from me and Brooke. I can't tell if she even noticed we were right down the hall from her.

I turn on one foot and follow Brooke down another hall.

"Can I come with?" I fall in step beside her.

She shrugs. "Free country."

The Georgia O'Keeffe campus is a lot bigger than Emily Dickinson. I imagine I'm a wayfinder, using windows instead of stars to navigate this strange and untamed continent.

We get to the doors to the library and Brooke hauls one of them open. She heads straight for the research labs and I see that one computer is down and two of the other three are taken. One of them holds the blue baboon bottom of one Inocente Doublefart Nevarez.

"Kyle! Brooke!"

We look at one of the other computers and see Cameron waving at us.

"He-hey! Cameroon Lagoon." I pretend not to even notice Ino and slap my books down by Cameron's station. Brooke pulls up to the other empty slot while I drag a chair over to Cameron's. He's looking at me like I just sprouted a third eye.

"Cameroon La*goon*?"

I smile at him, showing all my teeth. "Can I use your computer for like twenty seconds?"

"I doubt you could find whatever you're looking for that fast," he says.

"You doubt the Amazing Constantini?"

"Kyle." Cameron tilts his head. Still, he smiles. *Mua-ha.* A chink in the mighty armor.

"Well, what are *you* looking up?" I ask.

"Extra credit. For history. I'm writing an oral report on the Manhattan Project, but I want more information on molecular chain reactions."

"Oo-kay," I say, "I'm sure that's super gripping but can I please just look up one tiny, super-small, extra tiny, little word?"

"All depends." Cameron leans back and rests his fingers in a tepee. "Do you have hummus in your lunch?"

"How do you know I get hummus?"

"I saw it on your table the other day," he says. "But I noticed you didn't eat it."

I squinch one eye. Mom's always packing me stuff

like flaxseed crackers with hummus or spicy nori—for a snack! I'd give anything for a plain and honest Oreo for once in my life.

"I might have it again today," I tell Cam.

"I'll type in one search item"—he lifts a finger—"if you let me have your hummus."

"Sure!" I stop myself before saying he can take my hummus for the rest of the year.

"How do I know you'll keep your word?" he asks.

I roll my eyes. "I swear on my blue fedora," I tell him. "You will reach the shore alive."

"What?"

"Just look up Polynesian wayfinders."

"That's two words," he says. "Not to mention they're not small."

"Cameron."

"Type it, *Cam*eron," Ino says from his computer. "Else she'll punch you."

Oh, go take a leap through a flying donut, pimple puss.

"You punch people?" Cameron looks at me.

"She punched him." Brooke jabs her thumb at Ino without moving her eyes from her own screen.

"Look, just *type* already!" I say.

"Okay, okay."

Cameron opens up a new browser window, types in 'wayfinders' and starts to read from the first link.

"Wayfinding is a method for navigating open waters without the use of a compass, radio, sextant or satellites."

"What's a sextant?" I ask.

"I'm telling you guys are looking up stuff about sex," Ino says.

"A sextant"—Cameron sneaks an irritated glance at Ino—"determines latitude and longitude at sea."

"Doesn't matter where you do it," Ino says.

"Ino, just be quiet, why don't you?" I tell him. "We're tryna work."

"Oh, so this is work for your little club," he says. "I could have been in that club, but I'm not a nerdy *lo*ser."

"Yeah, you'd rather pick up people's gnarly garbage after lunch," I say.

Cameron covers his mouth as he tries not to laugh but out pops a rebel snort. Ino gathers his books and stands up from the computer. Here we go again.

"Already told you, Wonder Woman." He comes up to me and flicks my fedora to the ground. Brooke stops typing and fishes it up. "You better watch yourself."

"Well, now *I'm* telling," Cameron says.

Ino gets in his face and Cameron leans back a little.

"What are you going to tell, you little walrus butt whisker?" Ino asks.

"That you're threatening Kyle," Cameron says. Then he looks at Brooke. "There are three witnesses. And if

I had to guess, there are probably cameras in here, too. So *you* better watch *yours*elf."

Brooke hands me my hat.

"You guys are a bunch of nerds, babies and *los*ers." Ino stays in Cameron's face for a few seconds before backing away. "I don't have time for this. I'm outta here."

After Ino leaves, Cameron shudders. Then he scratches the back of his neck really quick and leans in to the screen to read more. "The wayfinder depends on the stars, the sun, the tides and other signs in nature for clues to direction," he says. Then he leans back. "You know what's odd?"

Brooke shakes her head.

"People like that guy are just as much a part of nature as the stars."

"You sure about that?" she asks.

"Think about it, everything has got to have a reason for existing," he says. "Not just the obvious things of beauty like the ocean and the moon but also things like mean people and—"

"Walrus butt whiskers," I say.

Cam laughs.

"No, I'm serious. They could be like mini antennas." I lift my index fingers and wriggle them.

"I just can't believe you actually hit that guy," he tells me. "He makes the Colossus of Rhodes look like Mr. Potato Head's little brother."

"Yeah, well, Reed told me not to let him bait me anymore."

"How do you mean?" Cameron asks.

I shrug. "I don't know. I guess kind of like don't let him get under my skin."

"I've always wondered what people mean when they say that," Cam says. "I mean, where does that saying originate?"

"I know where it comes from," Brooke puts in.

Cameron lifts both his eyebrows, waiting for her to go on.

"In the bad way, like you're saying"—Brooke nods at me—"it comes from supposedly evil spirits that used to tunnel into people's thoughts and make them do things they otherwise wouldn't do."

"Freaky fratelli," I say.

"But there's also another way," Brooke says. "A much nicer one."

Cam turns to face her.

"The other way that someone gets under your skin," Brooke goes on, "is when they share your heart. When someone gets under your skin in the good way, it's like their spirit talks to your spirit."

"Well, what if you don't believe in spirits?" Cameron says.

The bell rings and the three of us start to gather our stuff.

"Think what you want," Brooke tells him as she swings her backpack over her shoulder. "But in my experience, we find what we look for."

Or *maybe*—I think as the three of us go to our separate homerooms—like the amazing Polynesian wayfinders, we find what we've learned how to see.

★ ★ ★

"Today we are going to learn about controlling the axis of your adversary while protecting your own," Coach Yeung tells us as we're all lined up in our gym clothes.

Mine still don't fit. It's been more than a week and I haven't had that growth spurt Mom keeps saying is right around the corner. I'm still the same and these clothes are still massive on me.

"Turn and face your partners."

Reed and I look at each other.

"By touching the skin of your opponent," Coach is saying, "you can listen to, or understand, the type of force they are emitting."

"What's emitting?" someone asks.

"Think of the sun," Coach says, "and how it emits light. Each of us emits an energy and through the sense of touch, our nerve endings take in that stream of energy being emitted by another. The more you develop your awareness of that energy by practicing with your partner," he tells us, "the more you can read intention through touch. This goes back to the axis. Imagine a pole running head to foot through the person standing in front of you."

I look at Reed and picture a street lamp sticking out of his gym shirt.

"That is their axis. With contact, you can get a sense of which way the pole is tilting. Then you can use that information to your advantage during combat. But you have to remember that a person is never still during engagement. There are constant readings you can take to stay ahead of the moves of your opponent."

I wonder if that's at all like getting under someone's skin?

"If you can remember that the opponent you're engaging never stays the same, then your ability to advance, subvert and defend will evolve with the living fight. Then maybe"—Coach smiles his warm, buttery smile—"your inner ear will begin to catch a piece of the silent song."

Reed and I start. At first, I'm distracted by a billion little thoughts. Like everything that *didn't* happen between Sheroo and me this morning and how Mom never wants to just park it right there and listen to why I should be allowed to stay on NAVS. But after Reed comes at me a few times, it's like the brain below my neck takes over.

Reed moves his arms around me and I lift mine like

sails, using both to make big, flowy circles. I'm warding off Reed's hands but I don't feel like we're separate. First we're doing the same circle, then we start to do two circles at once.

Reed holds my gaze with his. I think about how way-finders use the shadows on the underbottoms of clouds to be able to tell if land is nearby. There isn't anything in the color of Reed's eyes that tips me off to what comes next, but I do notice that, behind him, the mats are stacked in fours and there's an orange volleyball sitting on top of one of them. There are no clouds in the sky outside the windows by the ceiling and when I glance at the ground during a really big figure eight, I notice one of Reed's shoelaces is broken. And, just for a second, the world isn't tugging away from itself at the edges anymore. Because it's like Mr. Arriéta told Meowsie on the very first day. Every thing is every things.

"Excellent, Kyle," Coach says. "Very well done, Youngblood. I think, as partners, you've had a moment and a breakthrough."

A moment and a breakthrough.

I'll bet not everybody has those.

"That a good thing?" I ask.

Coach tips his head the tiniest bit and looks me in the eye. "It's a very good thing."

"Coach."

Coach's assistant walks through the doors to the gym.

"Phone call," she tells him. "Yer sister."

Coach strides to the front of the room. "Okay, class, tomorrow we will be exploring the roll back and the press. But for now"—Coach motions to his assistant—"I'm leaving you in Coach Calandra's hands."

He tells her something then does a little jog to the door before disappearing into the hall.

"All right, kittens, listen up." Coach Calandra claps. "Coach Yeung has gone to take an important phone call and in the meantime, we're gonna have a little break and do somethin' fun."

A couple people cheer and the assistant coach grins.

"Anyone in this class know howta play"—she stops all dramatic—"Steal the Bacon?"

No one answers.

"Y'all don't know how to play Steal the Bacon? Well, saints above and beside, this is a glittering tragedy. You, there." She points at Donna.

"Donna," she says.

"Right, go and git a clean towel from the locker room, hunny." She claps again. "We're gonna cook us some *break*fast! All right, counting you off. One, two, one, two, one, two."

She goes through the whole class and separates us into teams. I'm a one and Reed is a two so we get sent to opposite ends of the gym. Marcy gets sent to Reed's side of the gym and Donna comes back with the towel and gets sent to mine. I look around at who else is on my side and see Ino Nevarez out of the corner of my eye. I don't want to stare at him straight in the face so I focus on the towel in Coach Calandra's hands as she goes over the rules.

"Okay, now, team one goes first." She points at Donna. "We'll start with you. Now, jest call out a name from team two and when you do, the both of you'll race to the center of the gym"—she straightens the towel and lays it right in the middle of the two teams—"to see who gits the bacon first. Then you race on back to yer side and the one who stole the bacon gits their team a point. All clear?"

Easy enough.

"Okay, Donna, you go on an' call out a name."

Donna lifts a fist to her lips and clears her throat.

"Reed!" she yells.

Quick as a flash, Reed starts running for all he's worth to the center of the gym. Donna starts like one second after he does and the lead he gets on her is too big so he grabs the bacon and starts running back. Donna stops in her tracks and Coach Calandra shouts at her.

"Well, go on, sugar! Don't throw in the towel!" She laughs. "Catch that old Thunderbird and getcher bacon back!"

So Donna guns it after Reed but, by then, it's too late. He's made it home safe and his whole team starts cheering and whooping and stomping.

Okay, I see how it's done. I stretch my neck and crack my knuckles and get on the edges of my feet, ready to fire the second my name hits the airwaves.

"Okay, boy, now it's your turn." Coach Calandra takes the towel from Reed and walks to the center of the gym to lay it down. "You call out a name and see if you can beat another member from team one."

Reed wipes his cheek with the back of his hand and hunches down like he's waiting for the gun.

"Kyle!"

I almost start to run before he even says it. It's like hearing him use my actual name instead of Fedora sends lightning through my legs. I'm pumping them as hard and as fast as I can with my eyes zeroing in on the towel in the middle of the gym. That bacon is *mine*.

Reed moves fast. Even though he just ran the length of the gym to beat Donna, it's like he has more energy and speed, not less. I'm looking at the towel but can feel him getting just as close as me. I pretend like there's an earthquake and the gym is cracking open like the crust of an overbaked pie. The bacon is actually my cat Circe so I dive to grab her and am already half turned around to run to my end of the gym when I feel the towel jerk back.

Reed's got it, too!

We grabbed the towel at the same time! I whip around and hang on with both hands but Reed is pulling from his end, just as strong. I lean back with all my weight but Reed digs in his sneakers on the gym floor and I don't budge.

Then I get an idea.

When he leans away in his direction I let go, just a little, and he tumbles backwards. Then I grab the towel even stronger and turn around to run with it like I'm home free.

But he's still holding on. I drag him a few steps before he gets his footing and starts pulling back in his direction.

"Steal the bacon!" everyone is yelling.

"Go, Kyle!"

"Get her, Youngblood! It's *yours*!"

Our sneakers are cutting into the gym floor and leaving scuffs all over the place when I feel Reed grabbing more of the towel with one hand over the other. He's pulling in closer with each grip and I can't move. All I can do is dig in my heels to stand my ground the way he was doing before.

He gets up close enough for me to hear him and says, "Surrender, Fedora."

"Death first!"

He laughs but grabs so much of the towel that all I have is a tiny bit left in my hands, which are all pink and a little sore from the struggle.

"Surrender," he says again. Then, he karate chops what's left of the towel between us and I feel the vibration all the way to my teeth.

I let go of the towel.

It drops into Reed's hands and he just stands there, shocked.

"Why'd you surrender?" he says, instead of running away with it. And I stand there, too, and stare at him.

"I know how we can lead Cameron out of the maze."

He smiles at me, breathless, while the sound of everyone else in the gym booing and shouting cutdowns fades into the walls.

"You do?" Reed asks.

"I do." I smile back at him.

Then I snatch the towel from his hands and sprint back to my side of the gym, outrunning the burning hot lava and doing a final, heroic leap over the line to rescue Circe to safety.

That night in bed, I'm on hyper alert as I listen for the sound of a bubble popping on my screen. I lie perfectly still in the middle of my covers with pillows standing on both sides and one on top. It's my fort. Even if it is a kind of saggy one. The room is all dark except for the light from the street lamp that's coming in through the shutters.

Marcy isn't interested in joining NAVS. She says she thinks there's a reason *I've* been picked for it, though—even if Mom has grounded me. She told me today that sometimes life is like a puzzle that you have to figure out. For example, why did I stand up for her? Why did I get a cool punishment instead of a crud-muffin one like pimple puss? And why, after everything, did I get grounded from the punishment that I now want?

I told her duh. Who wouldn't stand up for her? (She said lots of people.) And that I got grounded because—

See, that's the thing. I don't really *get* why I can't do NAVS. I mean, yeah, I should have told Mom we were getting into the pool at Donna's. (And that Mrs. A. wasn't gonna be there. I mean, I guess I kind of knew since Donna never had her check the note.) But, come on, *to*tally grounded for life because of that?

My screen bubble pops and I'm busting out of my fort before I even look at the avatar. When I do, it's not one I've ever seen before. It's a huge . . . shrimp.

MasterOfCeremonies: NAVS meeting tomorrow morning in the library at 7:45. Attendance a MUST!

I stare at the message for like five hundred lives. The meeting is in the library. During school hours when I'll *already be there, anyway.*

My fingers fly as they type a response.

the_amazing_kyle: who's the shrimp?
MasterOfCeremonies: That's a CAMARÓN, thank you
very much.

A dolphin avatar pops up on the screen.

Donita: be kind to your friends in the ocean.

I laugh in the darkness at Donna and Cameron and
something heavy—like a boot—thunks against my wall.

"Cut it out!" Roger yells. "I'm tryna sleep, you little
fart blossom."

Rog and his beauty sleep. I mean, come on, it's not
even nine. He's gonna make more noise than me and then
Mom'll come in here and ask me what I'm doing on the
computer when I know the rule is no electronics thirty
minutes before bedtime.

MasterOfCeremonies: We can't afford to waste any
more time. The experiments in the pool at Donna's
didn't get us any closer to figuring out a communication system. It's time to get serious, team.
Logan: agreed

Donita: not my fault.

MasterOfCeremonies: No one is blaming anyone.

But we either go forward as a team, or stop.

Logan: I vote go forward

I rub the tip of my nose. There's a milk shake in my stomach. All bl*waa* and bl*waaaa* like my guts are, I don't know, in a milk shake making maker.

A blender.

I glance at my closed door and picture Mom taking off her rings and rubbing in her night creams while Dad reads something off his tablet. (*He* gets to stay on electronics before bed.)

Okay, so how bad can it be, really? If I just go to the meetings before school? Because it seems like everything is falling into place without me even trying. And plus, if Sheroo's gonna be eating lunch with her new friends anyway, I might as well be hanging out with Brooke — where is she, btw? — and the NAVS team at recess, too. I mean, it just makes sense.

Put it this way: The competition in the Civic Center is still more than a month away. Which means there's plenty of time to help the team solve the maze without going to anyone's house behind my parents' back *and* find a way to let them know I never quit. Because why would I have gotten such an important clue to the maze during Steal the Bacon after Reed's and my moment and a break-through if I wasn't even meant to share it? Exactly.

Logan: so its settled. We'll see EVERYONE tomorrow
   at 7:45?

I push down the sour milk shake in my stomach until I almost can't feel it at all.

the_amazing_kyle: I'll be there.

Chapter Nine

I'm surprised how nervous I am as I walk to the library the next morning. I almost wish Sheroo would see me and make a scene or something so that I'd have an excuse to go to the bathroom. Then later I could say sorry! Couldn't come to the meeting because there was a crisis in the hall. You know how it is.

But the way is clear straight to the door from the moment Brooke, me and Reed get off the bus to the minute we walk in and see Cameron and Donna already sitting at a table.

"Good news, everybody," Reed says. "We think we've found a way to lead Cameron out of the maze." Then he turns to me and says under his breath, "Fedora."

Who, me? Wait, what are we doing again?

I stand with buzzing knees in front of Cameron, Donna and Brooke—all people who I *know* for a fact are smarter than I am—and then open my mouth to see what pops out.

"We need rope," I blurt.

Reed looks at Cameron then Donna and says, "Okay. Anyone know where we can fetch some rope?"

"From the Drama department?" Brooke says.

"Good morning!" Mrs. A. walks into the library. "Sorry I'm a little late. Please"—she rolls a hand—"keep doing what you're doing."

"Mrs. Arceneau, we need rope," Cameron tells her.

"Well, that should be easy enough," she says. "So long as you don't plan to plug it in." She smiles at her own joke then sets her bag on the table. "I expect we can go through the P.E. department to get that."

"Brooke was thinking props from the Drama department," Donna says.

"And what do we need the rope for?" Mrs. A. asks.

Everyone turns to stare in my direction.

"Yeah, what are we going to attach it to?" Cameron asks.

I take a breath. "You."

"You're going to pull me with rope?" he says.

"No, we're not gonna *pull* you with the rope." I shake my head. "I mean, what would be the point of just leading you around? There has to be some give and take," I say. "A message that we send so you can use your own head to think about it and react."

"And how are you going to use rope to send a message?" Mrs. A. asks me.

123

"I think we should actually *have* some rope," Reed puts in. "So she can show us instead of tell us."

What he said.

"Brooke," Mrs. A. says. "Why don't you and Kyle go to Miss Romero and see if we can locate some rope?" She turns to me. "How much do we need?"

"Enough to tie Cameron to another team member," I answer, "but also to leave room for someone else to stand in between."

Well, freeze my farts 'n' call me Elsa. I actually sound like I know what I'm talking about.

"Right. I'll head to the gym," Reed volunteers. "See if Coach might have some. We'll be back."

Reed, Brooke and me go into the hall that leads to the gym and the school theatre.

"I'm glad your mom changed her mind about letting you do NAVS," Brooke says as soon as we're out the door.

I swallow. "Well, she hasn't *exac*tly changed her mind."

"What do you mean?"

"I mean that, well, for now, I'll just be helping you guys while I figure out a plan."

"She got an idea in gym class yesterday," Reed tells Brooke. "And after the meeting at Donna's, I'd say the team needs all the good ideas it can get."

Reed takes a separate hall to go to the gym while Brooke and me pay a visit to the Drama teacher. No dice.

Thankfully, though, when we get back to the library, Reed is already there with a couple of jump ropes.

"That should work," I say.

I hope.

"I don't think we have time to try anything out now," Cameron says. "We have"—he looks at his watch—"two minutes and forty-three seconds before first bell."

"Forty-one seconds," Brooke says.

(I love Brooke humor.)

"Okay, so why don't we meet in the gym at lunch?" Donna suggests. "That way we can have as many jump ropes as we need."

I nod. Though inside, I'm beginning to realize what all this means.

I, Kyle Constantini, am gonna go to a bunch of meetings, help my team solve a maze and go compete at the Civic Center (the *Ci*vic Center!) all without telling Mom and Dad.

"Looking forward to your idea," Reed tells me as Brooke and I swing on our backpacks and get ready to go to homeroom. "The team needs a mind like yours, Fedora." Then he steps out of the library before us and heads down the hall to his locker.

Brooke looks at me, then at Reed walking away, then back at me.

"What?" I say.

She shrugs one shoulder. "Nothing."

★　★　★

Soon as lunch is over, me and Brooke head to the gym. Coach has left a pile of jump ropes on a fold out table and Mrs. A. is in the bleachers, grading papers and crunching on a pear.

"Kyle, you take charge," she tells me. "If you need me, I'll be right here."

Here goes nothin'.

"Okay, so do I tie the jump rope on?" Cameron asks.

"Give her a second to explain," Reed tells him.

"Go ahead and tie the rope to your waist," I tell Cameron. "And, Reed"—I look at him—"you tie the other end around yours."

By the time they finish, there's no room for anyone else to stand between them. They look awkwardly close together and like they're trying really hard not to think my idea is mouse poop.

"Why don't we use three jump ropes?" Brooke suggests. "Tie one around Cameron like a belt, one around Reed and then hook the third one between them to make room for the person standing in the middle?"

"Yes." I point at her. "That."

"All right, what now?" Cameron says once they've rigged the ropes.

"We're going to send a message to you," I tell him. He

126

nods. "Now pretend you can't hear or see. Brooke, can you stand by the middle of the jump rope between them? Reed, stretch it out as tight as can be."

Reed pulls as far away from Cameron as he can.

"Okay, Brooke," I say. "Give it a good chop right in the center."

I swallow. *Please* work.

Brooke hits the rope and everyone looks at me as I look at Cameron.

"What did you feel?" I ask him.

He doesn't answer.

I clear my throat. "Cameron?"

"I thought I wasn't supposed to hear."

"Okay, fine," I say. "Pretend like you couldn't see Brooke hitting the rope but pretend like you can hear me inside your head asking the question."

He takes a breath. "Okay, I felt a tickle."

"That's good!" I say. "A tickle is good!"

"It is?"

"Yes, because that tickle you feel is what we are going to use to send you messages."

"That could get confusing," Donna says.

"Yes, but that's why it's a challenge," I tell her, feeling just a *lit*tle more confident. I may not be the smartest scholar in seven counties, but I know a good idea when it kicks me in the bahamas. "Picture like this," I go on.

"We use the rope between Cameron and Reed to shoot different messages. One to tell Cam when he needs to turn a corner, one for when to stop, one for how many steps to take in a straight line, et cetera."

"Well, then I think we'd need more than one rope between them," Donna says. "*Three* ropes would make better sense. We can not only use different messages but send them through different ropes. One to send the message to turn right, one to send a message to turn left and one to send a message to walk forward."

"Donzie, you're a genius," I tell her.

"And we could have one person be in charge of the right rope and another person be in charge of the left," Brooke says.

"Wizard," I say. "So not kidding. You all could form a brain tank."

Brooke grins.

"You mean a think tank?" Cameron asks.

"Bings. Seriously, we could be the generation to save the universe from the stupocalypse."

Cameron lifts one side of his mouth in the kind of smile where you can see someone getting the joke a little bit at a time and then deciding they like it, so I smile back at him. Because the way I'm seeing it now, this is just as kick as giving him his own star chart to memorize. Except it's *we* who are Cameron's stars, and he's gonna learn to put his trust in us.

We're finding the right way to get under his skin.

September starts to melt away like a gooey marshmallow on top of a hot chocolate. The weather turns coldish and I'm happy to be spending the time after lunch in Mrs. A.'s classroom or the gym instead of outside where Reed says soon it'll be brass monkeys. (That's British for freezing.)

It turns out, of course, that it *would* be easier to just lug Cam around with the rope — and I can feel sometimes that the team wouldn't mind taking that route when figuring out our message system starts to get a little hairy. But I think that the way to make it through a maze is not just to have something or someone do all the work for you. It's important to be able to get a message, munch on it a little and then make a choice based on what *you* decide. Otherwise, it would just be a bunch of commands that you have to do no matter what. And I don't see where that would be the glory of solving a puzzle, so I try my best to encourage the team to keep thinking about how to work the ropes to send a clean signal — from one problem-solving mind to another.

Speaking of problems, Mom doesn't have a clue I've been going to the meetings. But that's under control because I've been planning to tell her at almost every dinner time. It's just that the right *mo*ment hasn't exactly shown up because she never went back to Braca Khan about the detentions and any talk of NAVS just sort of went away.

That night at the dinner table, though, I'm pretty much seven seconds from blowing my own cover. If I don't find a way to talk about everything that's been going on, Dad and Meowsie will end up having to peel bits of me off the cabinets while Mom calls Exploded Daughter Control.

"Michael, remind me of the date of your choir performance at the bank downtown," Mom tells Meowsie.

Everyone has been super into Meowsie's voice stuff while no one has the smallest idea about my team's amazing system of vibrating cables.

"You know there's an app for that," Dad tells Mom. "You can sign up for a lot of the activities the kids are involved in at all three schools and get updates sent directly."

"Kyle, pass the tomatoes."

Mom made fried green tomatoes as part of dinner tonight and they are 100% revolting. Tomatoes are always leaving bits of themselves like slug trails wherever they've been. Frying them green doesn't change the fact that they're the most barftastic food in captivity. But since tonight I'm frying my brains trying to think of a way to finally tell Mom and Dad my big surprise about NAVS, I think maybe I'll try the tomatoes.

"Nicki, for the love of my final taste bud." Dad clanks a fork to his plate. "Would it absolutely kill you to crush a handful of sea salt on these?"

He's taken a bite of the enemy. Maybe now is the time for a compliment?

"I like your hair today, Mom."

"Eat your food, Kyle."

Mom's distracted. She ignores Dad and pulls out her tablet.

"Michael, the concert."

"November seventh," he says, not looking up from his book.

"Time?"

Meowsie chews his bite and swallows. "Six."

"Thank you for not talking with your mouth full."

"Hey, Mom." Roger walks in and kisses Mom on the cheek. "You're looking swell." He smirks. "Have I told you that is the perfect color for you?"

Craptain Kirk. He must have something he wants to ask her for, too.

"No, you cannot go to Curt's house on Friday," Mom says.

"What? Why?" Roger says.

"Because we are all going to the cabin this weekend.

It's the last weekend before it'll get too cold to be agreeable."

"But why *this* weekend?" Roger wails. "We've been planning this party for weeks!"

Mom raises an eyebrow at him.

"Well" — my brother gets a sheepish look — "not, like, a *par*ty party. Just" — he lifts a hand — "a little get-together. For a couple of old friends."

"Is your old friend Sondrine going to be there?"

Roger scrunches his brow. "Sondrine?"

Mom smiles.

That's good. A smile is good.

"In any event, no," Mom says. "Not this weekend. I'm sorry."

Roger's arms hang at his sides as he slumps into his chair.

"Sit up straight, Roger," Dad tells him.

Roger sits up for like a second then folds his body over the top of his plate.

"Roger."

"Mom, I'm really looking forward to some nice family time at the cabin," I say.

"Yes, you may invite a friend." She looks at me and smiles again. "I've appreciated how well you've endured your discipline this month, Kyle. You didn't go behind Dad's back or mine and you stuck to your guns. I think that deserves a small reward. If you'd like to bring along Brooke or Sheroo, that would be fine by me."

I smile back at her but it's like someone has jammed toothpicks inside my lips to prop them open. Mom slides her warm hand over mine.

"You've been a good girl," she tells me. "And you're well on your way to earning back my trust."

She takes a bite of the fried green tomatoes and scratches the space between her eyes.

"Roger, pass the pepper."

I am a fly. I am a fly in a maximum-security spider web with a wing on the fritz.

Meowsie's been firing a jillion messages on Instant pushing me to pick Marcy to come with us to the cabin so he can talk to her about wayfinders. But I don't want to *hear* any more about wayfinders! Maybe some time away from all of this will clear my head. That's what stressed-out grown-ups do, right? Go away for the weekend so they can sit around in hot tubs while all the answers come to them?

Come to think of it, there actually is a Jacuzzi at the cabin. It's in the room with the windows where you can see all the pine trees. There's even actual bears. I can already picture one coming up to a window and resting his poor, tired paws on it. He's blind and can't hear and everyone's afraid of him but I just tap on the glass to communicate that we are his friends. There's a moment and a breakthrough with bears in all the forests of the world because of my new message system — which it turns out all animals understand because the only language you need to know is good vibrations.

I stare at the ceiling as another bubble pops on my screen. I'm about to message Meowsie not to ask me about inviting Marcy anymore but it's not even him. When I go to my screen to look, I see that it's Brooke!

(Hey, that rhymes.)

I yank out my chair and flop into it, scooting in close.

analog_girl: Bet you thought you'd never see me on here again.

the_amazing_kyle: Brooke what is going on??? Why haven't you been doing NAVS chats? You haven't sent even one message on Instant. You've been all mr mysterioso for like a month. Ever since the tests.

analog_girl: Have you found a way to let your mom know you've still been doing NAVS?

the_amazing_kyle: Negative. Plus Sheroo still isn't talking to me. I think she thinks I stole YOU KNOW WHO away from her.

analog_girl: Nobody steals anybody. People aren't passwords.

the_amazing_kyle: Tell her that. Brooke my parents are taking us to the cabins this weekend and they said I could invite a friend. I want to ask Sheroo to try to make up with her but I want to ask you too.

Logan: this doesn't sound like official NAVS business

My heart does this gigantic *floop* against the tops of my ribs, like someone just launched it in the air like uncooked pizza. Man, he has a way of appearing out of nowhere. He's like the Cheshire cat of the Internet.

analog_girl: I'm at my Dad's so I won't be on the bus tomorrow. See you at lunch.

the_amazing_kyle: Wait Brooke don't log off!!!!!!!!!!!!!!!!!

Brooke's little record player avatar goes into sleep mode.

Zoinks.

Logan: sorry

I let out a noisy breath.

Logan: but if you want my opinion Fedora you should ask your mum and dad if you can bring along both your mates

the_amazing_kyle: y?

Logan: just think you should

I scratch my arm and stare out the window, trying to think of what else I should say.

the_amazing_kyle: Reed do you even remember my real name?

I know he does, because he yelled it that one day in gym when we were stealing the bacon. But my breath still gets stuck in my throat as I wait for whatever he's gonna type next.

Logan: it's right there on the screen kyle

My heart goes unzipped as I imagine his voice saying my name again.

Logan: btw who's YOU KNOW WHO

Crap'n Crunch. Now, my heart is a bongo at a luau! Feel like I just chugged two packets of Fun Dip and washed it back with Orange Fanta.

the_amazing_kyle: Sorry Reed I gotta go. Im so
SORRY!!!!

I log off and shut down the computer before doing a
flying jump onto my bed. I fling the covers over my head
and do a little running in place before flopping down on
the mattress with a thunk. Then I jam my face into one of
my pillows and scream.

Enough is enough.

The next morning, I'm standing by Sheroo's locker
when she comes up to it by herself.

"Hey," I say.

"Hey."

We look at each other for a few seconds before something else to say pops into my head.

"Can I leave my math book in your locker?" I ask. "It's
closer to my class so I don't have to walk as far and I won't
have to carry it around."

When we were in fourth, me and Sheroo shared a
cubby hole. Supposedly you weren't allowed to share cub-
bies, but we did it behind our teacher Mr. Menchaca's back
and he never knew the difference. Or if he did, he didn't
care. Anyway, I'm hoping that sharing a locker—even

if it is just a math book—might jog Sheroo's memories about the good ol' days.

"Whatevs," she says now. "Guess you need my combo."

I lift a shoulder. "If you don't mind."

"Whatevs," she says again.

She teaches me her combo and pops open the lock.

"So," she starts with her back to me, "is Reed, like, your boyfriend now?"

I rub my nose.

"Well, *is* he?"

"No," I say. "Why would you even ask?"

She turns to face me. "So, then why do I always see you guys together before school and at lunch?"

I give an exaggerated shrug. "That's just for NAVS."

"Thought you were grounded from NAVS."

Guess she and Brooke are still talking. I take a breath and let it out.

"Listen, Sheroo, do you want to come with my parents and brothers and me to the cabins this weekend?"

She's quiet. But then she asks, "Is it the one with the Jacuzzi in the window room?"

I smile. "Yeah."

"And the bears?" She smiles, too.

"Uh-huh." I laugh. "So, do you think you can come?"

She sighs and her smile disappears like a puff of mist.

"It sounds like fun, but..."

"But what?"

"Sasha's having a party."

"Another one?"

Sheroo shrugs. "She throws them all the time. It's, like, every weekend, practically."

"Oh," I say, and then don't know what else to add.

"I already told Mercedes my stepmom would give her a ride."

"Right," I say. Though I have no idea who Mercedes is.

All I know is that my heart is a pancake. I never thought the day would come when Sheroo would be so booked up with other plans that there'd be no room left for us.

"So." She hugs her books. "You're not crushing on Reed, then?" And I can see all over her face what she wants my answer to be. What she needs my answer to be.

My hands start to sweat. I can't see a single way where I could be totally truthful in the middle of a hallway packed with a ton of people without risking a scene because, fine. Maybe she is a tiny bit right. Maybe I *do* like Reed in that way, after all. And o-*kay*. Maybe it's even possible I have for a while now. But it's not like I stole him from her. It's not like she walked into the Reed store, bought a Reed and then I went and snuck into her house and took him while she was fixing a snack.

Second bell rings. She's waiting for me to answer.

"I don't want us to be late," I say. "I mean, any more than we already are."

She looks away from me and shakes her head.

"Talk later?" I ask.

She nods but doesn't lock in a window seat on the 7:07.

"Sure." She slams her locker door. "Later." Then she turns and starts to walk to 6D.

I stand there in the hall as it empties out of everyone except the most tardiest of students.

I'm not ready for this.

I'm not ready for the freaking Grand Canyon to start opening up in the middle of one of my most important relationships in the world.

It's one thing to give Doublefart a righteous sock in the paunch when he's acting like a jerkface buffalo bahanka. But it's totally different to have to face the music in a win/lose situation with someone who used to be one of your very best friends.

Mom says it's okay by her if I take both Brooke *and* Marcy to the cabin because I've really turned things around. For a second I feel so stuffed with guilt I almost bust out a confession but then I stop. I mean, what is she, Father

O'Reilly? Plus a confession in the heat of the moment would ruin my plan to get Marcy and Brooke to help me figure out a way to let Mom know I've still been doing NAVS *and* to convince her to let me ride it out until the end. After all, a triple brain is like, what? Three times better than one brain. Right? Maybe more, if Brooke's brain counts for two. (Which, in my book, it does.)

I'm hoping me and my friends can sit at the very back of Dad's Denali but Roger gets there first—the tootweed. He's just like a boy cat, marking his territory. The whole back of the car already smells like Cool Ranch Doritos and his deodorant.

Meowsie tells him to please move so he can share the seat.

"Sit in the front with Kyle and her friends."

Meowsie glances at Marcy before just staring at Roger. Then, very quietly, he says, "C'mon."

Roger rolls his eyes and shoves over some of his stuff, giving Meowsie the teensiest-tinesiest spot. Barely enough to click a seat belt.

"Thanks," Meowsie mutters.

I feel like tagging Roger in the head with my sneaker. I think maybe I might, when he's asleep. Or maybe I'll just scoop out the lint between my toes with his toothbrush.

We stop on the way out of town at a drive-thru to get cheeseburgers and onion rings, which Brooke wolfs down like a person who's been living in a shack in the middle of no-man's-land for sixty thousand years. Has her mom gone vegan or something? Ms. Jeblanco has always been kind of an activist. But I guess that's because she spends all her life sculpting and artists are always getting passionate about something.

The road on the way to the cabins starts off all desertish but then little by little turns into the woods. I like watching it change. It's like moving into the green dimension. First there's shrubs that look like fat dwarfs with grass haircuts but then they start to turn into tall trees. Like they're all hunched together smoking bark cigars and wearing visors around a midnight game of seven-card stud.

When we get to the mountains where we have the timeshare, Dad says, "Well, everyone. I have a surprise."

All of us sit up a little straighter except for Roger, who's still sleeping with his mouth wide open.

"What is it?" Meowsie asks.

Dad grins in the rearview.

"Dad!" I grab the back of his seat and hang over it. "Tell us!"

"Kyle, keep your seat belt on," Mom says.

"It is."

She looks at me and sees that it's still on. Just a little loose, is all.

"Kyle, for pity's sake. Is that how you've been wearing it the whole time?"

"I can make it bigger or smaller." I pull it in and out to show her. "See?"

"Just sit back," she says. "Or else no surprise."

I slam back into the seat, shaking Roger out of dreaming the impossible dream.

"Dad, what's the surprise?" Meowsie asks again.

"We," Dad begins, "are going to be staying in a newer, nicer cabin. It's a condo, actually."

"Snowbird Heights?" Mom clasps her hands together and Dad looks at her.

"Snowbird Heights."

Mom squeals and unbuckles her seat belt to lean over and kiss Dad on the side of his head.

"Mom," I say. She looks back at me with a glowy face. "Seat belt."

She laughs and settles back into her seat with a click.

"What's so great about *Snow*bird Heights?" I ask.

"Well—" Dad lifts a shoulder, still smiling all proud. "I don't know that you kids will be able to tell much difference. It's just a newer place, nicer kitchen."

"So Mom can Gollum all the salt there."

"Well, that's the other surprise," Dad says.

Make it a good one this time, Pops.

"*I* am going to be doing the cooking this weekend."

Roger lets out a groggy laugh and a sniff.

"Thanks, Rog," Dad says. Then he looks in the rear-view at us again. "I've been taking cooking classes."

"You've *what?*" Mom asks.

"At Thyme and Again. I'll be doing the grocery shopping and cooking this weekend and if everyone likes it"—he tips his head—"maybe I'll cook more at home, too."

Mom looks gobsmacked—there's another word I learned from Reed. It means super surprised. I'm a little nervous that her feelings will be hurt but then she snuggles into the seat a bit more and I can see her smiling reflection in the window.

That's it, Pops. Soften her up. I'm gonna need all the cuddly Mom I can get when I finally grab my moment and drop the NAVS bomb.

Chapter Ten

The condo. Is. *Rad!*

At first, I thought Dad's surprise was lame but now I see why Mom was so excited. The room in the center has a fireplace—which Dad called it a kiva—and it's all huge with skylights and you can see the room on top! I mean, you can hang off the edge and look down on people and maybe toss stuff on them. As Brooke, Marcy and me race to the second floor, I think about how rad it would be to drop something on Rog when he's not looking.

"Kyle, be careful with the loft!" Mom yells.

"Okay!" I yell back. Even though I have no idea what a loft is.

"Just put your things in your room so we can take a nice walk to the shops while Dad drives Michael and Roger to get some groceries."

I can hear the pep in Mom's voice. This'll be great. She'll get herself a decoration or two for the house from the shops and be even more happy and then I'll start to drop hints about the importance of vibrating cables. I might even work up to it by bringing up the major problem of bear-to-human communications. It's the genius plan.

I hang over the side of the room and look down on Dad and Roger. Now I know how birds feel scoping out cars. I let my eyes move around the big, open den and wonder what I could bean Roger's head with.

"Girls, use the restroom and freshen up so we can go!"

And just as Mom says it—I mean, just like in the movies—Marcy tells me to come to the window.

"*Mo*-om!" I call out. "Snow!"

"What?" Mom cries, and we hear it all the way up the stairs. "Keith, you'll have to get to the store quickly to get all we need. Was this in the forecast?"

Maybe I can add mustard to Dad's grocery list. That'd be pretty easy to tag Roger's head with if it's the squeezie kind.

"What do you guys think about roasting hot dogs over the open fire tonight?" Dad calls out.

"What about marshmallows?" Brooke says to me.

"And get marshmallows!" I shout.

"Marshmallows," Dad says. "Great idea."

I can see him pull out a piece of paper and a pen to make a list. Roger says put down Doritos and Meowsie asks if we can get stuff for S'mores.

"Anything else?" Dad asks.

I hang over the edge like an opera singer.

"*Mus*-taaard!"

The whole night it snows. Meowsie finds out the coffee table is a chest that opens up and is full of board games. Some of them haven't even had the plastic taken off. We play one where you have to draw things and make people guess what you're drawing, but nobody draws that great so sometimes it takes too long to guess to be any fun. The best part is when we turn off the lights to roast marshmallows for S'mores and I get this fantastic idea. I grab Dad's flashlight and tell everyone to listen because I have an important safety message and turn the light up on my face.

"This is the story," I start quietly, "of the family who couldn't understand bears."

I wish I had some creepy sound effects to go with my important safety message but I didn't think that far ahead.

"Far away in a cave," I say, "lived an old, shrivelly woman who knew how to tap messages. But the shrivelly woman's mom told her she was not allowed to work on her message system. So she had gone to make her house in a cave."

"Thought this was about bears," Roger says all bored.

"For years," I go on, "the old woman's message system was not used and the bears in the county all began to come up to people's windows in the middle of the night and steal their pies." I lower my voice and make it all gravelly. "They especially loved huckleberry."

"Why do you have to use the flashlight? This isn't scary."

"*Ro*ger! I'm setting a *mood*."

"Well, get to the point already."

"Rog," Dad says.

Just wait until he gets up in the night for a glass of water or to take a whiz. Mustard city, baby.

"Only the woman's message system could stop the bears from stealing huckleberry pies," I say. "But no one really cared about that. They just started making cherry."

Roger yawns.

"But *then*," I say with a fierce voice, "the bears began to find a way into people's houses and steal their pants. Dads had to take out the trash in just their underwear. And you could see their brown socks pulled all the way up to their hairy knees."

Marcy and Meowsie laugh.

"And older brothers couldn't go out on dates!" I point a finger. "Because none of the girlfriends wanted to be seen with a guy in just boxers with funny short guys wearing beanies."

"You wear boxers with weird men in beanies?" Dad asks Roger.

"They're not beanies, they're *fezzes*," Roger answers. "And they're worn by Shriners in this edgy cartoon that's really popular online."

"Yeah, Shriners sound totally edgy."

"Look, can we just get on with the story?" Roger looks at me. "Else the shrivelly old woman is gonna have a rock rolled over the entrance to her cave."

"It's not a story," I say. "This is for safety. Of *e*veryone you love."

"And their pants," Brooke adds.

"Just wrap it up, Kyle," Mom tells me. "I think everyone's about ready for a movie."

After the movie—which had Humphrey Bogarts and was boring and super long and even made Mom cry a little in the one part where Ol' Humphs comes back to tell the main girl that he will never forget her—everybody except the parents fights over the sink in the one bathroom to brush their teeth. Mom and Dad don't have to wait their turn because they get their own sinks—two!—in the master bedroom. That's always been a funny thing to me, the master bedroom. Like it's the ruler of all the other bedrooms.

You must give me the spring-fresh sheets — straight from the dryer — and the only night-light that still works!

But why?

Because I am the Master!

Brooke and I finish up and wait for Marcy to carefully clean her hearing aids before we all go into the bedroom at the corner of the condo. It's a crazy-rad room. With a mondo three-sided window ledge and a skylight in the corner. We all agree to keep the blinds open so we can watch the moon shine all over the freshly fallen snow.

There's two twin beds and a big open space by the window. I let my friends have the beds and grab some comfy-cozy blankets from the hallway closet to make a fort on the ledge. Except that it's not a very good fort. More like a nest but whatever.

"Did you hear that?" Brooke whispers.

"What?" I say.

"This!" She grabs my shoulders and roars in my face.

"Girls!" Mom yells from the master bedroom after my scream. "Lights *out!*"

I have to admit that was a good scare. Not that it was well planned or anything. It was just good because it worked. We click the door to the bedroom shut so Mom and her jumbo sonic ears won't pick up every sneeze.

"Who wants to go back into the kitchen and get more marshmallows?" Brooke says.

Marcy gags. "This late at night?"

Brooke climbs into one of the beds and leans back on the pillow with her arms behind her head. "It's never too late for marshmallows."

And with that, I'd have to agree.

I lean back on the ledge by the window as a big white chunk slides off the roof and makes a plonk as it hits the ground. After Marcy switches off the big lamp, she pulls out a flashlight to light up our faces.

"Let's tell scary stories," Brooke says.

"I don't really like scary stories," Marcy puts in. "Unless they're like Kyle's and are more funny than scary."

"What about you?" Brooke asks me. "Tales from the dark side, yea or nay?"

"I like spooky stories," I say, snuggling into the covers. "And if we wait for like an hour, I'll get up with you to go get more marshmallows."

"Okay then, how 'bout Truth or Dare?" Brooke suggests. "Kyle, you go first."

"All right," I say, "truth."

"Okay." Brooke props her head on one hand.

She's got her crazy curls up in a ponytail on the top of her head and her shadow looks just like a monster. But it's a cute monster. Because it's Brooke.

"Do you —" she starts.

"No, I get to ask the truth," I say.

"No," Marcy tells me. "You *chose* truth, so one of us gets to ask you."

I roll my eyes in the light of Marcy's flashlight. "Fine," I say. "Go ahead and *pick* my brains, why don't you."

"Do you," Brooke says, "have a crush on anyone this year?"

Go for the jugular.

"Can I pick Marcy to answer first?"

"Nice try," Marcy says.

"Well, *do* you have a crush?" I ask her, even though I kind of can already guess. Starts with an M, ends in an E and has EOWSI in the middle.

"Kyle, c'mon," Brooke says.

The truth is I've never been the type to share my crushes. Because, even if my friends don't like the same guy that I do, what if the person I trust all of a sudden cracks under the weight of my confession and stands up in a crowded room to yell, 'Kyle has the screaming hots for so-and-so!' Then I'd have to walk around for the rest of the year in dark glasses and a mustache.

I cross the fingers on both hands under the covers. "I don't really think I have a crush on anyone this year."

"Kyle," Brooke says. "This is *Truth* or Dare."

"Fine, Chris Dixey," I say.

"Who's Chris Dixey?" Marcy asks.

Brooke bolts up in her bed. "You have a crush on Chris Dixey?"

I turn my head to look at her. I swear, it's like her curls got even springier in the last five minutes. She looks almost electrocuted.

"Why?" I ask Brooke. "You think Chris is a grossening hog breath or something?"

"No," she says quietly.

"All right, well, I said my truth," I tell her. "What's yours?"

The room is totally silent.

"Brooke."

She clears her throat.

"Just that Chris gave me his email before he moved," she says.

My mouth goes dry.

"So, did you write to him?" I ask.

"I wanted to," she says. "He wrote me a couple of times."

"Well, why'd he give *you* his email?"

I can't believe this. Here Brooke hasn't been on Instant but she's been secretly keeping in touch with Chris Dixey and his hydramatic freckle. I'm totally and completely speechless.

"I don't know," Brooke says. "I guess maybe he had a little crush on me? I don't know."

Oh, I think she knows.

"Brooke, why didn't you tell me this before?" I ask.

"Well, why would I?" she says. "I mean, it's not like I knew *you* had a crush on him. You're not like some people who have 'Sheroo Youngblood' signed all over the inside of their binder."

James and the Giant Crud Bomb.

"So, did you write Chris back?" Marcy asks Brooke.

"I might have written an email or two."

"Why'd you stop?"

For a second, Brooke is quiet.

"My mom's been kind of, I don't know, having problems."

Now Marcy and I both sit up, her in her bed and me on the ledge.

"What kind of problems?" Marcy asks.

"She's been having a lot of tests run because she gets nauseated and her head hurts all the time," Brooke says. "She even gets pain in her muscles and feels really tired."

I sink against the pillows and stare at the ceiling with a cold pit in my stomach, thinking about Donna's mom.

"But what does that have to do with emailing Chris back?" Marcy says.

"Her naturopath thinks it might be EHS."

EHS?

"What's EHS?" I ask.

"Electromagnetic Hypersensitivity Syndrome. It means she might be allergic to Wi-Fi."

"You mean, like, the Internet?" Marcy asks.

I had *no* idea people could be allergic to the Internet. "So that means you can't—"

"Write emails to anyone. Or chat. Least not in my house."

"Well, why did *you* have to have tests run?" I ask.

"They were trying to see if whatever was wrong was genetic," Brooke says. "But it turns out I'm not allergic to Wi-Fi. I only have a mild allergy to kiwi. But my mom still chucked a ton of electronics from the house anyway. She won't even let us use an Ethernet cable. She says all screens leak radiation and the more you're exposed to, the worse it can get."

"So, that's why you haven't been on NAVS chats?"

"That's why I haven't been on anything. Or why my mom didn't get me a phone this year like she said she would before Dad left. We have a landline again."

"What's a landline?" I ask.

"It's a phone you hook into the wall."

"But how do you carry it out of the house?"

"You don't," she says.

"Well, has getting rid of the electronics helped your mom feel better?" Marcy asks.

"I don't know," Brooke says. "A little, I guess. I don't know."

"Brooke, I'm so sorry," I say. I can't believe Brooke's mom gets sick from the *In*ternet.

"I did read an email from Sheroo at my dad's," Brooke says.

"And?"

"She asked if you're really on NAVS. I told her you've been coming to the meetings but that I don't know if your mom is going to let you compete since technically you're not allowed to be on the team."

"You *still* haven't told your mom?" Marcy asks me. "You are adventuresome."

"I'm not adventuresome." I roll onto my back and lay flat on the ledge, trying to stare past the pinkish night clouds out the window and straight to the stars. "I'm a tropical fruit basket with jicama for brains. Which you've already picked. I'm a picama brain." I turn my head to face them. "You guys have to help me figure a way out of this. It's been driving me crazy for, like, years."

"Years, Kyle?" Brooke says.

"You should invite Mrs. A. over for dinner," Marcy tells me. "Invite her to your house and have *her* tell your mom all the wonderful things you've been up to."

"You know, that's not a bad idea," Brooke puts in.

"There's no way the team would have gotten this far with the solution if it wasn't for you."

Hmmmm.

"But you'd better do it quick because we have only like, what? Three weeks until the challenge?"

"Two."

The more I stare at the ceiling and turn it over in my head, the more I think Marcy might be a pure and simple Einstein. I mean, maybe if I *did* invite Mrs. A. for dinner and she started bragging to my family about how well I've done with NAVS, Mom would feel pretty bad forcing me to back out after that.

I could bring it up tomorrow, once Mom gets something nice for herself at the shops and is in a snazzy mood. I imagine myself in one of those old monster movies where the camera starts to close in on the main scientist's sweating face and he says in this big, shaky voice, 'It's got to work. It's just *got* to.'

"So, do you really have a crush on Chris Dixey?" Brooke asks me.

Good ol' Christopher Dixey. Wonder if his freckle's even flirtier in Helena.

"Not really," I tell her. "To be honest, I guess I'm kind of over him now."

"Well, just so you know, I wouldn't have emailed

him if I'd known you were in love with him," Brooke tells me.

"But I thought you said people aren't passwords," I say. "I mean, it's not like you would have been stealing him from me. After all, you're the one he gave his address to."

Fair's fair.

"I know," Brooke says after a little bit. "I wouldn't have *tech*nically been doing anything wrong. I guess people just have to work out their own values. And I think, according to mine, I wouldn't have written him if I'd known all along that you liked him."

"Values," I say. "You mean, like a code?"

"I guess."

I lie perfectly still in the half darkness and pull the blankets up to the bottoms of my eyes. Whenever I come to the cabins, I have this terrible fear that a daddy longlegs will crawl up my nose while I'm sleeping and lay eggs in it.

Values.

Mine are all totally bent up and . . . oh, who am I kidding? I don't even *have* a code. Unless my code is to do what you gotta do in the moment and then worry about the consequences later.

Truth or Dare can be kind of a crud-muffin game sometimes. I'm not even in the mood to tag Roger with mustard anymore.

Chapter Eleven

The shops. Are so. *Bor*ing!

I *hate* the shops! Not even having Brooke and Marcy with me is making them fun because we have to walk like fifty jillion blocks to go into what looks like the same store with the same decorations for the house over and over and over. I'm pretty sure I'm going to melt into a quiet puddle of desperation, right there in front of one of the cash registers, when something catches my eye.

It's a magic kit. With a picture of a wand and scarves of all different colors and a trick card set with trick dice on the box and everything. I wanna look inside so bad I peel back the top a little—it was already kind of opening—and try to slide a pinky through. I've always wanted to be a magician. Well, I mean not always, but maybe I should explore the possibility now.

"Hon, ya gonna pay for they-at?"

The lady behind the register has hair in a pinkish

bun with huge, rolling bangs. She's snapping a piece of gum and has gigantic boobs with a religious necklace kind of squishing between them.

"Cuz if ya ain't gonna pay fawr it, ya caint be openin' it."

I hug the kit to my chest. "I'm thinking about it."

"Well, think 'bout it with yer head, sugar pie, not with yer hainds."

I nod and rush off to find Mom. As I turn the corner to get away from the amazing Madam Raspberry, I come face to face with the worst possible nightmare of all imaginings and horror.

Mom is talking to Mrs. A.

Mrs. A.!

Of all the boring shops in all the mountain villages of all the world, my NAVS sponsor had to walk into this one.

I creep up behind a shelf of garden gnomes and peek over the red pointy hat on one of them.

"Kyle has been doing very well this term," I hear Mrs. A. telling Mom. "She's bright and engaging and consistently warm with the other students in the class."

"Well, that's certainly good to hear," Mom says. "After our bumpy beginning."

Pleasedon'tmentionNAVSpleasedon'tmentionNAVS pleasedon'tmentionNAVS.

"Well, a lot of good has come out of that rough start,"

Mrs. A. says. "She's really impressed us with her engineering ingenuity."

Ingenuity? What's ingenuity? Since when am I an engineer?

"I think a lot of the work done by the NAVS members has developed because of a seminal idea Kyle contributed early on. Together, they've made wonderful progress with the mechanism she and the other students have since refined to guide one of their own through the maze."

There's this terrible, horrible, terrible quiet right after Mrs. A. stops talking. I squeeze my eyes shut and wish I had paid attention that one time Mrs. Ockfatrea tried to teach me how to pray the rosary.

"I'm sorry," Mom says in a funny voice, "but did you say—"

I know it's desperate.

I know it's crazy and that I can kiss my magic kit buh-bye if I go through with what I'm thinking, but I really don't have a choice. As fast as I can, I scramble to the top of the tallest gnome on the ground and balance on his blue shoulders. Then I open my mouth to shout the one thing that will stop the conversation between Mrs. A. and my mom from growing one. More. Word.

"BEAR!"

I've never been kicked out of a store before.

But what's worse is that Mom was asked to leave, too. I've never seen a face so red in my entire days on this earth. I would rather have been in the path of a mutant tomato waiting to roll over me than to be staring down Mom.

Marcy says what I did was bonkers but Brooke thinks it was kick. All Dad said when he found out what happened at the shop was, "The jig is up."

All that night and the whole ride back home the next day, Mom barely speaks to me. She hardly even looks at me. Roger lets Brooke borrow one of his mp3 players so she's listening to music almost the entire way, while Marcy teaches Meowsie sign language as they play everlasting Uno over the seat. I have a lot of time to think things through and here is what I come up with.

Number one, I shouldn't have pretended to see a bear and scared all the customers. (Even though watching Madam Raspberry choke on her gum *was* classic.) Number two, I really should have told Mom like a billion years ago that I was still doing NAVS. Even if it was only at school and *tech*nically, I am free to roam anywhere I want between classes on campus.

Which leads me to number three: I'm sick of being grounded and I don't want to spend the month of October the way I spent September.

Number four, that's probably not up to me. What *is* up to me is what I do from now on.

It's time for a code.

Obviously, I can't keep ghosting the meetings. I'm gonna have to choose. If Mom ever talks to me again I either stand up to her and tell her I'm going to keep helping the team—even if she won't let me officially participate—or I stop. But I'm not going to keep things the way they've been. I once heard someone on a talk show say that you have to own your choices and I had no idea what the schneck they meant then but I think maybe I do now.

It's not that I all of a sudden think it's fair that Mom grounded me from something I'm good at just because I biffed it a couple times at the beginning of the school year. But, looking back, I guess I also don't think it was the best idea in the entire kingdom of ideas to play Powerball with the facts.

I look out the window and watch the trees morph back into grumpy green dwarfs.

Even though I'm determined to come up with a code and really stick to it, an eensy part of me still wishes I could pull a Freaky Friday and trade spots with Brooke right about now. It'd be so much easier.

I'd even wear her old stripy pants.

When we get home, Mom is still acting like I'm mold. The boarder staying with Marcy and Brooke's dad come to pick them up and Mom is all teeth and politeness, but as soon as she shuts the door on everyone, it's like I'm not alive. I almost wish she'd tell me what my punishment is going to be and just get it over with. This calm before the storm is making me want to run around the den with my hands over my head yelling, 'The British are coming!'

I go into my room and see that a whole NAVS chat happened over the weekend while I was gone. It's still up on my screen. I drop my bag of dirty clothes on the floor and pull out the chair in front of my computer.

Donzie: last two weeks before competition. anyone have anything they want to bring up at the meeting on monday?

MasterOfCeremonies: I definitely do. First order of business is to finalize what we're going to strike the cables with.

Donzie: cameron's right we can't hold off on that any longer.

Logan: I wanna hear what fedora has to say

MasterOfCeremonies: Kyle?

I stare at the bag of laundry with my fedora tossed on top and think about the hats worn by the good guys in the Wild West. What does Fe*dor*a have to say, anyway?

Do I keep helping them? Do I stop? *If* I keep helping them, I'm going to have to sit down and have a talk with Mom and Dad about how I haven't gone to anyone's house but that I *have* been going to meetings before first bell and at recess.

I wish Mom would listen.

I wish I could actually show her all the work that I've done. It's funny because here I am working on a communication system and I haven't communicated with her at all.

There's gotta be a word for when stuff like that happens.

I start to write a message to Meowsie on Instant.

the_amazing_kyle: hey what's it called when say for example you own a coffee shop and you're allergic to coff

"Kyle, your father and I need to speak with you."

Mom knocks softly and I scratch my neck. I cross my room and open the door.

"In the kitchen," she says. I stare at a bloop of mascara on one of her eyelashes and swallow. "Now."

I follow her down the hall to the stairs. Her footsteps

are all soft on the carpet. I keep my eyes on the ground and just feel really, really sad. I'm not going to be able to compete in the challenge. Will everyone else be forced to give up my ideas since I'm not an official member? Will they be mad at me? Brooke and Reed knew all along I was doing everything behind my parents' back but will Cam and Donzie ever forgive me?

As Mom and I enter the warm, goldy light of the kitchen, I see Dad. He's sitting at the dining room table with a cup of hot tea. I can see the steam coming off the top in little curlicues that get all relaxed before they disappear.

Circular power.

I glance up at Mom. She looks tired from all the driving and probably all the thinking. I never wanted to use my circular power to mess with her center of gravity. I'm just sorry, is all.

"Kyle, I think you know the basic issue that's at stake here," she says.

I nod but, really, I have no idea what the basic issue at steak is. What does that mean, anyway? I look at Dad's tea, feeling hungry.

"I think what Mom's getting at," Dad says, "is that the main thing we're dealing with here" — he tips his head a little then lifts a few fingers from his mug — "is trust."

I scratch the tip of my nose. Why in the world does everything itch all of a sudden?

"When we send you on the bus to school," Dad says, "we trust you'll come back on the same one."

"Dad, that was just—"

"Let your father finish, Kyle."

"When we send you to your classes," he says, "we trust that you're not going to hit people."

I take a breath and shake my head. Have I ridden the wrong bus home or punched *one* single bully since the first week of school?

"When you say you're going to a meeting for a club," Mom adds, "we trust that you're not sneaking off to a swimming party when you're supposed to be grounded."

"Mom." I feel like I'm gonna cry. This is *so* unfair.

"Kyle, the entire month of September, you were participating in something that I told you was off-limits."

"But, Mom—"

"Just listen, Kyle," Dad says. "Right now, silence is your strongest ally."

Silence? Are they serious?? Are they *still* not going to listen to me?

"Mrs. Arceneau had a lot of complimentary things to say about you but you seem to look for ways to cancel out the good," Mom says.

Forget Exploded Daughter Control. If I have to sit here at this table and listen to all of this without being allowed to say anything back, we're gonna need state-of-emergency money from the government to put this kitchen back together.

"Kyle."

I look at my dad's face. He's pretty handsome for an old guy. And he doesn't even really look that old. My brain starts running fast. Dad said silence is my best ally but maybe my *real* best ally is sitting right in front of me.

"Your mom and I aren't trying to make your life miserable."

"I know," I say, even though I only half believe it. "But Dad, it's just like the salt."

"The salt?" Mom and Dad say it at the same time.

"Yeah, the salt," I say. "Mom thinks it's super bad for you but without it at all, the food tastes grotesque."

Mom cringes and I wince.

"What I mean is" — I swallow — "it's not like salt's the enemy. It's the way everything comes together."

Mom and Dad look at each other but don't say anything so I grab my chance and run with it. Hard.

"Mom doesn't want to put salt on the food because she cares about her family. But there's more to health than just doing all the right things separately. It's the big picture. Why live forever if you're going to be eating food that makes you wanna blow chunks?" I take a quick breath. "You have to look at every side. It's important to be healthy but part of being healthy is being happy. Which is why you're learning to cook, right, Dad?"

"What does this have to do with you lying about NAVS?"

"It's important for you to be able to trust me," I say, "but it's also important for you to *act*ually trust me."

"Kyle, you repeatedly violated that trust." Mom raises her voice.

"I know, I know," I say, and feel so many different emotions, tears start to form a line in my throat. "The problem is two things. I didn't tell the whole truth."

"That's a pretty big problem," Dad says calmly.

"But you wouldn't listen," I tell them. "Afterward, I couldn't explain to you that we were going to work on echolocation like with dolphins in Donna's pool. I didn't bring a towel because I was afraid you'd think it was a swimming party but it wasn't. I'm sorry about that. But the truth is Mom got there right at the moment when we'd gotten in the water. It *was* a NAVS meeting."

"Without a sponsor?" Dad raises both eyebrows.

My head falls back. "*Why* do parents think that kids can't get together to work without having someone telling them what to do?" I ask the ceiling.

"Well, you weren't working," Mom says, still kind of loud. "You were having a water fight and you were grounded!"

"We started *out* with a water fight." I look at her. "Don't you guys have bagels before business meetings? I mean, can't people warm up to work?"

"Kyle—" Mom lifts a palm. "You have been going behind our backs for a *month*."

"I know."

"That's not trust!"

"I know! But can't you see it works both ways?"

Mom wipes her face and gets up to grab a mug from the cabinet.

"Kettle still has water," Dad tells her.

I like that Dad knows how to get mad without getting mad. I love him for it. I wish I was more like him in that way, actually. Then I wouldn't even be in this stupid situation. I could kick Ino for having started this whole mess by being such a jerkswirl.

"Can I at least tell you about our vibrating cable system?" I say.

Mom takes a breath and lets it out with her back still to us. She's at the stove pouring water for tea. I could go for a hot chocolate right about now. My stomach makes a noise like it agrees.

I look at Dad and he nods so I shove away thinking about food. Both my parents are quiet for a lot of minutes while I explain everything to them from the very beginning. I tell them about how Cameron won't be able to hear or see in the maze and that he has to trust us to guide him. I tell them about how Meowsie's wayfinders spend their lives working on their deep awareness of the natural world and the motion of the earth beneath their feet — or actually their boats — and how the things I learned from Marcy and Coach Yeung have helped me understand we don't just see with our eyes and hear with our ears. We can use everything. Our skin, our memories, the things we think are gonna happen or hope are gonna happen. We can use all of that to navigate the dark places. And we can use each other.

"So what does this have to do with cables?" Mom sits down with her swirly hot drink. I watch her blow the steam away and take a tiny, testing sip.

"At first, Donna was the one that started us thinking on echolocation," I explain. "But when that didn't really help at the pool meeting, I had a moment and a breakthrough with a game in P.E. because we were looking for a way to communicate to Cameron without using batteries or electricity. It had to be something that didn't need extra power."

Dad gets an interested look on his face.

"All of this was because of what Marcy was teaching me about how she hears through her fingertips and . . . other parts. And me and Reed were learning about sending and receiving messages through the skin in gym."

Mom gives Dad an alarmed look.

"It's t'ai chi, Mom. It's nothing bad. It's the ancient martial art."

Dad smiles at Mom with his eyes, just like Reed used to when I first met him.

"So at the next meeting, we all worked together to come up with the three-cable system to attach to Cameron. After that, we came up with the taps to send messages for when he turns left or right or stops or how many steps he moves forward."

"How does he turn a corner if the cables have to be stretched to tap them?" Mom asks.

"Reed is attached to the cables on the other end and one of us taps the left and another taps the right. When it's time to turn a corner, the one on that side taps once and we let the cables go loose so Cam can navigate the turn. Then Reed moves to make them tight again and we tap the middle to let Cam know how many steps to take until the next turn."

"What are you using to tap?" Dad asks.

I shrug. "That's part of what we're"—I stop— "I mean, *they're* going to try to decide on Monday."

I almost can't believe I'm backing down without a fight. I had actually been thinking about standing up to Mom and Dad and telling them that I was gonna keep going to the meetings during school even if they wouldn't let me be officially on the team.

I don't have it in me to fight my parents, though. I just don't. Either I can get them to see things my way or I stop forcing it. And that's when it really gets clear for me. This isn't about salt or skin or bears. It's about stars.

The stars move and the earth moves and we move and we have to look for when things are moving our way and hop on for the ride. You can't shoot down the stars. You have to learn them and feel them and watch how they rise, and trust.

"I'm so sorry I lied," I tell them.

And right as I hear the word coming out of my mouth, I realize holding back any part of the truth is pretty much the same thing as a lie. It's only easier to kid yourself about it.

"It felt really, really good to be the one who came up with the first solution for the team and it would feel even better to be able to finish what we've started and actually compete in the maze. But I'm not going to do it if it means I have to fight you or go behind your back," I say. "All I can tell you is that this is something that has become important to me and that I want to be there for my team. That I'm sorry and I want a chance to do things right."

There. All said.

That wasn't so horrible, actually.

Dad does this tiny smile but Mom lets out a tired sigh and wipes her mouth with one hand. She and my dad look at each other but don't say a thing.

"Go get cleaned up and ready for bed," she says. "And turn off that computer. I don't want you on it at all tonight."

I look at Dad.

"Do as your mother says."

I get up slowly from my chair. "What about dinner?" Inquiring stomachs want to know.

Mom finally gives me a small smile. "Get your shower," she says. "Then come down and you can have something."

"No salt," Dad says.

"Shut up, Keith."

Mom swats at Dad and he smiles.

"I'll have something ready for you, Kiki," Dad tells me. He hasn't called me that in a really long time. Like since before summer. "And tell your brothers to come down to eat, too. But *aft*er they've gotten cleaned up. You kids made my car on the way home smell like bear."

Mom and I both look at Dad, then each other. I'm freaked Mom will remember how mad she was when I got her kicked out of the boring shop but then she starts laughing. Like full-on cackles from the rowdiest member of the studio audience.

I leave the kitchen and go straight upstairs for a shower. I swear, parents are super fruit loops sometimes. Fruit loops with boots and a cape.

Chapter Twelve

Dad makes these tasty sandwiches and vegetable stew, but we're all too tired to do any more than eat and go to sleep afterward.

Well, not really.

I lie in bed and squeeze my eyes shut so I don't have to stare at the ceiling. There are horses up there. It's like the chariots are on tonight. When my eyes were still open, I think I could even see some spit roping from the mouth of the second horse. She really wants the trophy or whatever the winners get. A nice, fat wreath for her long, proud neck and a crunchy bucket of apples and orange sugar cubes. If they have orange sugar cubes.

I still haven't answered the chat. I'm too scared to tell the team I can't help out anymore. I'd hoped that maybe when I went back downstairs after my shower, Mom and Dad would say, 'Great news, Kyle. We're so impressed by your determination to make things right we've decided to let you do NAVS, after all!'

But they didn't.

We didn't talk much or laugh or anything. Just munched our yummy sandwiches and then everyone brushed their teeth and went to bed. Mom and Dad to their master bedroom, because they're the masters.

The next morning when I wake up, I have the heart of a robot. Dad makes this rad blueberry salad with crumbly cheese and almonds in it and I shovel mine down and barely remember to say thank you. All I do is:

O-pen mouth.

In-sert bite.

Wipe lips.

Do not feel mad. Do not feel sad. Do not feel bad.

As I'm waiting for the bus, my arms and legs are all buzz town. It's a terrible feeling. Wish I could turn into a pterodactyl and fly over to a tsunami somewhere. I'd rather be swooping down to load innocent bystanders onto my back for a few hours instead of this.

"Kyle!"

A horn beeps twice and I spin around to look.

It's Dad!

"Get in the car, Kiki," he says through the window.

I shade my eyes from the crackling autumn sky. "I don't understand."

"I'm taking you to school today," he says. "We need to talk."

I look at the couple of other kids waiting at our stop then climb into Dad's passenger seat. I click the belt and face the front, feeling even more jumbly than before.

"I have an idea about what you could use to tap the cables," he tells me as we start to drive off.

"Wait, what?" I pull out the seat belt and lean forward so I can look at his face. "Does this mean you and Mom—"

Dad nods. "This means me and Mom."

"Oh, Dad!" I roll down the window and scream out of it. Mom would have freaked, but Dad just laughs. "Sorry. Had to get that out."

Dad chuckles into the rearview.

"Hang on, one more."

I stick my head out and scream again but this time there's a lady in a teal jogging suit walking three dogs. She jumps and says a cuss word at me.

"Dad, can we *please* go back to the bus?" I ask.

"Why?"

"Because I wanna tell Reed and Brooke I don't have to hide anything from you guys anymore!"

"Well, don't you want to hear my suggestion about what to tap with?"

"Oh." I settle back into the seat. No sense rushing.

I mean, I can always tell Reed and Brooke the good news at the meeting in the library. If I don't *explode*! "Of course."

"Just joking, I don't have a suggestion." Dad smiles. "Just thought that was a good opener."

"Are you kidding? It was killer." Then I do my trademark click and wink and look out the window at the beautiful world.

★   ★   ★

Sometimes in life, really good news is followed by really craptacular news.

When Mrs. A. tells us that morning in the library that the school can only send four of*fic*ial members to the challenge—and that it turns out I haven't been of*fic*ially signed up since Mom spoke to Principal Brac in the beginning of September—she lets us all know that I will be the one she adds to the team as an alternate.

An alternate.

Which means unless lightning strikes one of my team members and turns them into a human electrical box, I.

Can't.

Play.

"You know I actually just got official permission from my mom and dad to be a part of the team this morning?" I tell my friends after Mrs. A. leaves.

"Well, that's ironic," Cameron says.

And there's the word.

Here's what I've decided.

I've decided it doesn't matter. It doesn't matter that, of-*fic*ially, I'm now just an alternate because, really, I'm lucky to be a part of this at all. I'm still on the team. I still was the one who came up with sending messages with vibrations. I still helped to develop how we send those vibrations and I can still help the team decide what to use to send them.

So, see?

All that really matters is that the team wins. Because if we win, we all win together. Just because I'm not actually *in* the maze with my teammates doesn't mean I'm not a part of the big Navsbowski.

This is what I keep telling myself as Marcy and I sit together at lunch. Okay, so I *kiiind* of moved away from Brooke and Donna, just for today, because all they wanna talk about is the challenge in a couple of weeks and I could use one minute of my entire life without being ob*sess*ed by NAVS.

"Hey, Fedora."

Reed slams a tray with what's left of a sloppy joe and milk on the table next to me.

"Time to get you sorted and here's how I see it."

Get me sorted? I need sorting? Reed casts a glance over his shoulder at Donna and Brooke then looks back to me.

"This whole NAVS business hasn't been easy for you from the first." He lifts his hand. "But, so what? Did you know that at my old school things were so skint half the class had to sit outside?"

"Reed."

He puts a hand over his chest. "Dead serious. But only in late spring. Look, I know it seems I'm taking the mick but the truth is, people all over have it rough. I mean really rough."

"I know," I say. Because I do.

"And I'm feeling for you," he goes on, "I really am, but sitting away from your mates 'coz listening to them talk about the challenge is hard for you isn't gonna help."

"Reed," I say again. Mostly because I don't know what else to say. Plus, I'm a tiny bit embarrassed that he's giving me this sorting talk all out in the open and right in front of Marcy. I mean, *she's* the one who's really had to build a bridge over troubled water this year.

"You're a fighter, Fedz," Reed goes on. "You face things and you don't run away. And you know what you've got to face now?" he asks.

I shake my head.

"Now that your mum and dad aren't giving you

180

something to push against, 'coz I know that's how you like it best."

I swallow and blink.

Holy mustard cannoli. Could he be right??

"Now, it's yourself you gotta get in the ring with," he tells me. "You gotta take that big, heaping spoon of disappointment and swallow"—he takes a slurp from the little red carton and crushes it—"and we'll all be the better for it. The team'll always need you, Fedora." He wipes off his milk mustache and smacks his lips before picking up his tray. "No sense backing down now."

He gets up from the table and moves away.

For a second, I can't face Marcy. I can feel her eyes trying to sneak under my fedora but I can't seem to get up the guts to return her stare. After about a minute, though, she just tells me what she wants to say.

"Being an alternate's not the end of the world."

Inch by inch, I look up. "I know."

"Can I be honest?" she says.

That question is never followed by something that's easy to hear, is it?

"I think Reed's half right," she goes on, "about you not being the type to run away."

I sit there, still, waiting for her to go on.

"It's like you don't run away from the big, in-your-face things," she says.

"Like Ino?"

She nods. "But the smaller things, that are kind of bigger in their own way, it's like they have more of an effect on you." She crosses her legs on the bench and gets comfy. "I'll try and explain. On my first day of school here, I was so nervous about whether or not these hearing aids were going to be a good walking stick."

"Walking stick?"

"Yeah," she says. "You know, like a blind person? They use a stick and it sends them information about the world. A curb, a chair, anything that they would have to sense first and then steer around."

I lick my lips, paying attention as hard as I can.

"In the school that I went to before, we didn't need walking sticks. Because that world was set up for people who couldn't hear. Everybody lip-read. Almost everybody signed. And everybody understood how it was okay to sometimes slip into your own place and not communicate anything at all. Here"—she looks around—"it's a totally different world. It's a world for people who have built-in walking sticks. They can hear. They take it for granted that everyone is on the same wavelength. But not everyone is. Some of us need help to be like everyone else. We have to work harder to understand and be understood. We look for people who will go out of their way to be nice instead of mean. Or better yet, people who don't make us feel like they have to go out of their way at all. Like you."

I blink. Me?

"I think the reason you get me is because you know what it's like to have to work a little harder to be understood."

"What do you mean?"

"Like with going behind your mom's back. Or being on the outs with your popular friend, Sheroo. You've got all kinds of guts when it comes to dealing with creeps like Ino or even a bossypants like Donna. But when it comes to what's really in your heart, it takes more work. More risk. And I understand that. I don't have a problem with being deaf. There are parts of it that I actually like better. It almost feels like a special power to be able to have the world go quiet so that I don't have to fight to make out my own thoughts. It's being in a world made for people who *can* hear that makes me feel like I'm on some kind of battlefield sometimes. See what I'm saying?"

I wish I did see everything that she's saying. But I think it's going to take me a little time to get it all sorted—as Reed would say.

"Use the part of you that is strong to help the part of you that is weak," she says. Then she knocks her shoulder next to mine and almost bumps off my fedora. "And go to it." She reaches out to fix my hat. "Slugger."

★ ★ ★

The next two weeks are almost the best of my entire time so far at Georgia O'Keeffe. Pretty quick it stops to matter that I'm not going to be in the maze because the people from NAVS headquarters or wherever it is send the school practice blindfolds and earplugs just like the ones Cam will use on the day of the competition, so everything starts to feel really real. Coach even has his last gym class set up some practice lanes so that we can actually guide Cam through them every day after school!

The first time he rocks the earplugs and blindfold, he starts falling to the side when he walks. Actually, he can't *stop* falling to the side. Even when we hook him up to the skinny braided steel cables — which is what we've settled on in place of the jump ropes — and attach him to Reed. I tiny-sign my name in the air to tell my left from my right and notice Cam goes to the right every time. His body just seems to wanna lean like that, which makes keeping him inside the lanes even more of a challenge.

The Wednesday before the competition, Ino and his buddies are in the gym after school because they're jerky lard buckets and have nothing better to do with their lives than watch us practice and throw shade at Cam.

"Little baby can't walk!" Ino calls out. "Poor little baby, just learning to take his steps, and he keeps falling."

His friends laugh and give him five, but Cameron doesn't notice because I guess he can't hear with the plugs. And obvs, he can't see.

We've decided to use a wand to tap the cables. It gave us the perfect excuse to get a magic kit with the school's money but what's really kick is that it works the best of all the things we tried. Spoons, rulers, backscratchers— Donna even suggested a tree branch—but nothing made a better walking stick than a magic wand.

The other thing we figure out once Cameron is wearing the belt, the cables, the blindfold and the earplugs, is that we can't just keep tapping the middle cable to keep him moving in a straight line. After you tap it enough times, even with the wand, Cam can't tell the number of steps anymore. The message gets too blurry. So Reed says what if instead of Donna or Brooke tapping the middle cable, they pluck it? But then Brooke goes well, how will Cam know when to stop? And that's when Donzie comes up with the genius plan of holding the cable.

"Do what, now?" Brooke asks.

"Hold the cable," Donna says. "You interrupt the wave."

Donna taps Cam on the shoulder so he can take the plugs out.

"Reed's gonna keep the cables tight while Brooke plucks the middle one," Donna tells him. "Then, when it's time to stop, she'll hold it so it'll stop vibrating. That lack of vibration is how you know when to stop."

"Can you show us?" I ask.

"Reed," Donna says, "tighten the cables."

He gives her a quick salute and stands as far as he can from Cameron.

"Brooke." Brooke looks at Donna. "Pluck."

Cameron laughs a little.

"Now, hold," Donna says.

"How?" Brooke asks.

Donna grabs the middle cable.

"I can still feel it," Cameron says. "Isn't it supposed to stop moving?"

Brooke uses her hand, too.

"Now it's stopped," Cameron tells us. "Okay, so then we need both of you to hold the middle cable when it's time for me to stop. Nice work, Donna."

Donna's cheeks go pink. It's the first time I've seen that color on her all year.

Cameron puts his earplugs in and the blindfold back on. Then we try it again. It works the first time but then after a turn he starts to tip to the right again.

"Ooh, look at the baby!" Ino sucks his thumb and waddles on the bleachers. "Poor little baby!"

Ino keeps saying the same stupid thing over and over until I feel my fists go white. I start to move in his direction but a hand on my shoulder stops me. I turn around and see that it's Reed.

He interrupted the wave.

He's followed me a couple of steps across the gym with poor Cameron attached to him. Cam's not able to see or hear so he's stumbling around with Donna helping him not to fall. And when I notice my team behind me, I think about the cables holding us together that we can't see but that are still there.

"Pick your battles," Donna tells me. "Too much at stake."

Cameron turns his head all over the place with the blindfold on. "Guys," he says. "I have no idea what's happening."

Brooke tugs off Cam's blindfold as I lean in toward Donna.

"What does too much at steak mean, anyway?" I ask her under my breath.

She smiles. "It means know when not to act like a blue baboon's butthole."

I look back to where Ino was goofing off on the bleachers and am surprised to see Coach Yeung standing near him. I can't hear what Coach is saying but ol' Ino is having a staring match with the ground. After a few seconds, he looks up at Coach and does this huge sigh. Then he nods one time.

As the team keeps working on the pluck and hold, I

can't fight my curiousness another minute so I tell them I'm taking five and make my way over to Coach's tiny office. I knock on the open door.

"Coach?"

My voice has a frog in it so I clear my throat. Coach stands up from his desk. Well, not really a desk. More like a card table with just a grade book and a bamboo in a pot.

"Kyle, come in."

I step inside the office and can hear my teammates laugh. I want to turn back to look but don't. Instead, I just clear my throat again.

"Coach, I was wondering," I start, "I mean, I know it's none of my business."

Coach lifts his chin a little.

"I was wondering if you could tell me what it was you said to Ino. Just now. I mean, what did you say to make him quit calling Cameron names?"

Coach looks at me with those dark, steady eyes of his.

"I asked him what he wanted to do with the power he's been given," he says. "I told him that he is strong in body. Not everyone is as strong in body as he is. He has the build of a leader, and I wanted him to think about what he was going to do with that gift."

"So, what did he say?"

Coach rests on the edge of the table and crosses his arms.

"I could tell you," he says, "but if it's all right, I'd rather

188

answer with this." He leans forward a bit. "You are strong in spirit. Not everyone has a spirit as dynamic and humane as the one you have been given. Inside you, lies the power to be the captain of your heart." His eyes go soft at the edges. "What do you plan to do with that gift?"

Chapter Thirteen

I'm standing outside my parents' room trying to work up the courage to knock.

I need to ask permission to go to Brooke's house tomorrow to spend the night. It's the Thursday before the Challenge and Brooke has invited Donna and me for an official NAVS slumber party on Friday before the competition. She says her mom will drive all three of us to the Civic Center Saturday morning. We're planning to make secret bracelets to tuck under our sleeves that only we know about. It's our sign for 'unbreakable team' and we're gonna give Cameron and Reed theirs when we meet up with them in the arena.

I take a shaky breath and lift my fist to the door but then let it drop.

What if Mom thinks I've already gotten to do enough stuff and says no? I mean, two weeks ago I wasn't even allowed to go to meetings for NAVS and now I wanna go to a slumber party?

Thing is, I'm a little scared that Mom will get mad if I even ask. Even though it's been pretty calm the last two weeks. No bears.

I plug into the source of my power and knock.

"Yes?" Mom's voice comes from the other side.

I twist the knob and the door creaks as I open it. But what I see when I peek inside makes my jaw scrape the floor.

"Mom, what on earth are you *do*ing?"

"Trying on my costume," she says. "For Halloween."

I take a few steps inside and move cautiously to the creature that is supposed to be my mother.

She has two faces.

On one side is her real face with this beautiful pointy mask over her eyes that glitters in the light. On the other side of her head there's this second face that's this like fire-breathing dragon thing. It's a mask but it really looks like it's breathing fire because the flames coming out of the mouth on the dragon side totally sparkle.

"What," I say, amazed, "are you supposed to be?"

"Just an idea I've always wanted to try," she tells me. "I first came up with it in my Psycho-Cybernetics class in college."

I move up to her and touch one of the flames. "What's a psycho cyber—"

"Careful, Kyle. This took me a long time to make."

"You *made* this?"

Mom looks in the mirror and smiles under her pointy-eye mask. "Do you like it?"

"Like it? Mom, I love it! That's the raddest costume I've ever *seen*! But... what are you?"

She lifts a shoulder. "It's something I made up," she says, "to explore this idea that, no matter how hard we try to avoid it, we're always struggling against the split in our hearts. Where we say one thing and mean another. Or promise one thing, but then end up doing the opposite. Even to ourselves. Especially to ourselves."

I swallow as she looks in the mirror and cocks her head.

"It came out all right."

"It's beautiful, Mom," I say. And mean it. "Are you gonna enter it in a contest?"

"Your uncle Jack is coming over to take you and Michael to the carnival while Dad and I go to a get-together. In all likelihood, there will be a costume contest."

I like it when Uncle Jack comes over. He's super relaxed and always wears flip-flops that show his hairy toes—even when it's freezing outside.

I pick up a grapey ceramic cat off my mother's vanity. I'm always finding this crazy, interesting treasure in all her things. Usually something small enough to hold in one hand and from another country.

"Cute," I say.

"That's a maneki-neko," Mom tells me. "A

192

beckoning cat. Commonly believed to have originated in seventeenth-century Osaka. It's from Japan."

"What's it beckoning?"

"Um"—Mom screws up her mouth and looks at the ceiling—"the truth is I didn't realize the different colors had meaning when I bought it. I just really liked that shade."

"So each color beckons a different thing?"

"According to custom," Mom says, "yes. Gold is wealth, I think. And black wards off evil spirits."

So they won't get under your skin.

"White is good health and pink is love. I forget what the red one means."

"Well, what about this guy?" I turn the cat to look at Mom. He's all roller-poller and jolly.

"Don't quote me"—she nods at him—"but I think purple means friendship."

I stare at his cute little paw.

Hi, friendship. Come home.

"Would you like to have it, Kyle?"

I look up at her and cup him just under my throat. "Really?"

She gives me a nice half smile. "Sure."

"Oh, Mom, thank you!"

I give Len a kiss between the tiny ears. (His name is Len.)

"Why'd you come in here, anyway?" Mom goes back to admiring her work in the mirror, adjusting one of the flames behind her. "Was there something you needed?"

I lick my lips. For a second, I'd forgotten all about Brooke's slumber party. Seeing your mom dressed up like a psycho cybernetic can do that. I high-pinky Len's paw and go for the gusto.

"Brooke's having a slumber party tomorrow for me and Donna because the challenge is Saturday and her mom will take us to the Civic Center after we have a nutritious breakfast and we're making bracelets as a secret sign for the team to say that we're unbreakable, so can I go?"

I can see myself in Mom's mirror, balancing on the very tips of my sneaks with my hands around Len like a prayer. She looks at me there and slides off her pointy mask.

"Yes, Kyle. You can go."

"But, Mom, it's just — wait, what?"

"You can go to Brooke's house for a slumber party." She turns to face me. "I've been thinking a lot about what you said. How trust is something that has to be in evidence from both sides and I think this is another good opportunity for me to extend some of that trust, to you."

"Thank you, Mom," I say. "Thank you so, so, so, so much."

"You're welcome, Kyle."

I slip out of her room and slide the door shut, thinking ol' man Courage has been kinda workin' for me lately.

I glance at the li'l guy in my hands and know just what I have to do.

★　★　★

I haven't used Sheroo's locker for my math book. I haven't used it at all. But the next morning during homeroom, I take Mrs. A.'s hall pass to go to the bathroom. I don't, though. I go straight to the locker.

I'm nervous as I work the combination, afraid I won't be able to get it right since I've never done even a practice run. It pops open on the first try. The locker door cries in the empty hall as I let it fall open.

Sheroo's not one of these throw-in-all-your-crap-and-slam-the-door types. Everything is in order. She even has a little shelf with tiny drawers and stickers of pegasuses (pegasi?) and little bean-shaped guys. One of them is jogging and another one is smelling a daisy. Maybe I should expand my sticker collection from just bats.

Okay, focus, Kyle.

I pull out the sparkly envelope and my little friendship cat, to beckon friendship back. At first, I'm just going to pat his head for luck and then put him back in my pocket but then I feel this little tug from the house of my power. I look at Sheroo's perfectly ordered locker and see a space right between some spirals and her Physical Science textbook. Len would fit perfect in there.

I slide in my note — a good-hope invitation — and place the jolly kitty right on top, for safekeeping. He's so adorable. I feel a pang letting him go but hope that, by leaving him in Sheroo's locker, something else good will come back. Hopefully, Sheroo.

I shut the locker door and click the lock.

I've done all I can.

Brooke's house always makes me think of art class. I think it must be stuck deep in the curtains or something because when I get there on Friday night, practically every room smells like turpentine and clay.

"Kyle, darling, come in," Brooke's mom says. She seems to have more grey hair mixed in with her brown now. It's pulled back into a sleek bun that shows off her tiny, twinkly earrings. When she moves out of the way so I can step in, I hear that it's not just Donna that's come over. Cameron and Reed are in the den, too. My eyes get all huge and I look quickly at Mom, wanting the chance to explain that I didn't know this was going to be like a *par*ty party. I hope she doesn't hear the guys and march me right back down the steps outside to the car.

"Mom," I say quietly as Brooke's mother glides toward the den in her skinny jeans, flowy sleeves and bare feet. "I didn't know Reed and Cameron would be here, honest—"

"It's all right, Kyle," Mom says. "I called before we came over. The boys'll be here for pizza and snacks and you girls will get to bed at a reasonable hour. Tomorrow's a big day and tonight"—she tips her head—"well, it seems like a good night for celebrating. You've all worked hard."

I give my mom a quick hug and run my overnight things upstairs to Brooke's room. She's set up two sleeping bags and Donna has tossed her stuff by one of them already so I get the one by the window—which is how I would have picked it. There's a tree right by the pane and it's breezy out so maybe Brooke'll let us crack the window so we can listen to what's left of the leaves on it. Plus, it's the full moon—or almost full. It really feels like fall now. All spooky and snugs.

"Well, what's *your* favorite Halloween candy?" Cameron is saying when I come around the corner into the den.

"Donno," Reed says. "But a good toffee apple always tastes ruddy amazing. 'Specially with jimmies."

"You mean a caramel apple?" Donna asks.

I shoot a quick look at the space where the TV used to

be. There's just this humongous sculpture of a crane. It's turned to the side and is showing just one eye. It's weird because Brooke's house actually does feel like it's missing a hum or something. Maybe not. It could just be my imagination. Or maybe it has a different kind of hum. Because Brooke's mom has hung a lot more plants everywhere, so it's definitely more mystical and junglier.

I go to the table set up with snacks and grab some carrots and celery sticks with plenty of dill dip. I love crunchy veggies so long as there's dill dip. The doorbell rings.

"Pizza!"

Brooke's mom pays for the delivery and we dig in like Martians who've just discovered the marvels of junk food. Cameron even doubles up two slices in a pizza sandwich and has to open his mouth kinda wide just to cram it all through. Everybody starts to talk about what it'll be like in the maze tomorrow and I think about how different it is when we're all talking about NAVS in person instead of on chat. Of course, we hear more from Brooke. Actually, I've kind of noticed that Brooke shares her ideas a lot more when Sheroo's not around.

It's strange, thinking about what Meowsie said — how some people bring out different sides of you that don't exist when they're not there. I wonder if it's the same when certain people *are* around. Do other sides of you disappear? Have certain parts of me disappeared since

Sheroo and I have been on the skids? A little ache blows up like a balloon in my ribs, right where my heart should be. It's not the kind of emptiness you feel when people move to Montana. It's the kind you feel when people are right where they've always been but still seem far away. Sheroo still hasn't answered my RSVP and tomorrow's the big day.

(Hey, that rhymes.)

We finish the pizza then go outside to jump on Brooke's trampoline. It's a little bit freezing but you can't really jump with a coat on so we just have to keep moving. Turns out Donna can do pretty amazing flips—forwards and backwards—so I ask her to show me how. Brooke gets in on it, too, and she's good!

"All right, lemme try." Cameron moves his arms out like he's trying to clear space for himself. As if one of his flips would knock us all to Osaka.

"You gotta tuck in more," Donna tells him. "That's the only way you're gonna be able to land on your feet."

"Well, maybe I don't want to land on my feet," Cameron sniffs.

"Maybe you'd want to if you learned how, mate," Reed says.

"Just, everyone move back."

Cameron flaps his arms out again and starts to jump as Brooke tugs on my sleeve.

"What is it?" I ask.

She moves her head for me to get off the trampoline with her so after she leaps off, I follow. The dry grass hurts the bottoms of my feet since we're just in socks.

"Is everything okay?"

"Everything's fine," she tells me.

"Your mom's not getting a reaction to someone's phone or anything?"

"No, nothing like that," Brooke says.

Reed and Donna are laughing and I get the urge to turn around and see what Cameron's doing but I don't want to be rude. I shake a hand to encourage Brooke to hurry and get whatever it is out.

"Kyle, Sheroo wants to accept your invitation to come to the maze tomorrow but she feels weird about it."

"Why?"

"She says you refuse to be honest with her about Reed."

Snap, crapple and pop.

"What does she mean, I re*fuse* to be honest?"

The truth is, I just really need to hear someone else's take on this whole thing—namely Brooke's. I mean, on the one hand, she's the one who told me people aren't passwords. But then on the other, she said she wouldn't have written Chris Dixey back if she knew I was in love with him. So, where do you draw the line on how much to share about what you're really feeling—and do some situations make that line go berserk?

Brooke takes a breath. "She says the main reason you fought to stay on NAVS is because you knew that was the only way you could spend time with Reed without making it seem like that's what you were doing."

I press my face together with both palms and groan. Okay, well at least *that* I know is totally grape nuts. I would have kept going to the meetings even if Reed hadn't been on the team. It felt good to be able to work a puzzle and come up with a solution. Good to do it because I wanted to and not because someone else was telling me that I *had* to. Being able to get to know Reed better was just a kick bonus point. (All right, very kick.)

"Is that what you think?" I ask Brooke through squashed lips.

"No," she says carefully. "I think Sheroo's the one who's not thinking straight because the simple fact is she likes Reed and he doesn't like her back."

I drop my hands from my face and sneak a look at Reed. He does an almost perfect flip and Donna cheers while Cameron tells everyone to move out of the way so he can try again.

"Why do you think Reed doesn't like her back?"

Brooke pulls me farther away from her trampoline.

"Because," she says, "I think you're the one Reed likes."

My heart creeps up into my trachea. The smell of smoke from someone's chimney hangs in the air and, usually, I like that smell. Right this second, though, I'm finding it a little hard to breathe. But that doesn't stop me from wanting to take a running jump onto Brooke's trampoline and doing a leapfrog over her house.

"Tell the truth," Brooke says with a serious face. "Have you and Reed kissed? Or anything like that?"

Okay, now the world has gone mad.

I drag her by the sweater sleeve even more far away.

"What?" I whisper fiercely. "Are you *crazy*?"

"So, you really are just friends?" she whispers back.

"Jiminy Crix, Brooke, yes! Of course we're just friends. And what in the world makes you think he likes *me*, anyway?"

"It's just that"—she stops and licks her lips—"he's always going around saying the *team* needs you."

"Well, doesn't it?" I say in a small voice.

"Yeah, of course." She does this big nod. "For sure, it's just"—she stops talking and starts to chew her thumbnail before spitting out a hunk of cuticle. Gross. "I think what he *really* might be sayi—"

"Scuse me, scuse me, scuse me, aah-ba-ba-ba-baa!"

Brooke and I leap back as Cameron pushes past us and heads straight for the sculpted bushes at the edge of her yard.

"Oh, my *word*," Brooke says as Cam heaves up his pizza sandwich.

She and I both hold on to each other and inch away from the scene of the crime.

"I'm getting my mom." She books it into the house.

"Cameron," I say weakly. Then he ralphs up what he had for lunch. Yesterday.

It's starting to smell. I take one huge step back to wait for Brooke's mom. Then I go inside, too, to see if I can find some paper towels.

"He just started puking out of nowhere," Brooke's telling her mom, who's wiping her hands on a dishrag as she heads out the door.

"Brooke, get a towel and a cup of water," her mom says.

"I'm on it," I say, and go straight for the towels I know are in a cabinet by the sink in the kitchen. "You get the water," I tell Brooke.

By the time we get the towels and the water to Cameron, he's a groaning, pale mess. His hair is plastered to his forehead and he's sweating. Honestly, I never thought I'd see him look this untidy.

"Brooke, honey, call Mr. and Mrs. Pinzón and let them know I'm driving Cameron home. The rest of you get inside and play a board game or something until I get back. He only lives a few blocks away so I shouldn't be more than ten minutes."

Brooke nods.

Reed, Donna, Brooke and me step inside behind Cameron and Brooke's mom.

"Lock the door," Brooke's mom tells her, then she leads a dizzy, miserable Cameron out the front gate.

Brooke clicks the door behind them and we watch out the window as her mom drapes a towel on the floor of the passenger seat and gently guides Cameron in, buckling his seat belt.

"Call his parents," Donna tells Brooke.

She goes to the phone and, just as she's about to pick it up, it rings.

Landlines are loud.

"Hello? Yes, Mr. Cooley. Yes, I understand. Right away, just—yes, okay."

She hangs up the phone and dials Cameron's number. I'm surprised she has it memorized. I guess with landlines, you can't just save people's numbers, you have to actually learn them.

She waits for the Pinzóns to pick up.

"Who just called?" Donna asks.

"Mr. Cooley." Brooke swallows. "Our neighbor. He says the smell is getting into his yard and that we better clean it up immediately. Hello, Mr. Pinzón?"

Reed pulls his phone out of his pocket and dials.

"David," he says. "Listen, mate, I'm gonna need you to come now."

Okay, this blows me out of the water. From everything I've learned about Reed, I never would have dreamed he'd be the type to bail when things got weird.

"Bring some of the sawdust," he adds under his breath.

Sawdust?

"Just do it, please. All right."

He slaps his phone and slides it back into his pocket.

"What was that all about?" I ask him.

"Just asking my brother to help me clean up after Cam," he mutters.

"You and your brother just *happ*en to have a bag of sawdust lying around?" I smile.

He doesn't smile back.

"It's trickier than you think, Fedora."

I let my smile fade so he doesn't think I'm doofing around.

"Try me," I tell him.

His eyes stay on mine for a few seconds. Then, his shoulders slump and he does this tiny, serious nod.

"Someday."

Late that night, Brooke, Donna and me are upstairs in Brooke's room, lying in our sleeping bags and staring at the ceiling.

"Poor Cameron," Donna says in a super quiet voice.

"I can't believe he threw up so bad," Brooke says. "I mean, he was fine the whole night until just at the end."

"I can't believe Reed and his brother cleaned it up," Donna says. "Much as I like Cameron, I don't think I could have done that."

"They were fast, too," Brooke says. "And thorough."

"How do you think Reed learned to clean up puke like that?" Donna asks. "And from the *bush*es, for crying out loud."

"Cam didn't do it in the bushes," Brooke says. "He hit the edge of the gazebo."

Donna's phone dings—are me and Brooke the last people on *earth* to not have their own phone?—and she slips out of her sleeping bag to get it.

"There's a message from Reed on Instant!"

Brooke and I jump out of our sleeping bags and run to Donna, face all green by the light of her screen.

(Hey, that rhymes.)

Logan: cam down for the count. just called his house
and he's got the flu thing going round

"Poor Cameron!" Donna cries.

"Donna, can you please keep it down?" Brooke looks at

206

her door all nervous. "And I want you to turn off your phone as soon as this conversation is over."

Donna looks at Brooke. "It's not like your mom has to know."

Donzie: What else?
Logan: hang on a se
Logan: sec

Brooke chews her lip and looks at me.

Logan: he isn't too happy about not being able to
   compete tomorrow
Donzie: so what are we going to do?
Logan: well

Reed's first word comes in but it takes a while for the rest of his message to pop through.

Logan: isn't this what an alternate's for

Donna and Brooke look at each other then at me.

Logan: you ready to try on some ear plugs and a
   blindfold Fedora?

Chapter Fourteen

The Civic Center. Is *huge*!

Everything feels electric. Like every person in the place is connected by a cable that's snaking a zap through the entire arena.

I'm nervous. Like, *ner*vous nervous. But I can't let it show because now the team is *really* depending on me and we have to do the best that we can. Last night after Brooke finally convinced Donna to turn off her phone, we ended up making something else instead of the bracelets. We're still the unbreakable team but now we have even more of a reason to fight for the number-one spot so we designed shrimp tattoos for our faces. Well, Brooke's mom did, anyway, since she's the artist. But we gave her design the team stamp of approval so now we're wearing them on our cheeks. They're not real tattoos, just face paint. Brooke's mom is going to do Reed's face, too, soon as we see him.

Coach Yeung is in the audience along with Chewbraca.

So is Marcy with Meowsie and Mom and Dad. And of course Brooke's and Donna's dads and David Youngblood. I scan the seats for Sheroo but haven't spotted her yet.

We've just been issued the official earplugs and blindfold and — thank God! — each entire team is allowed to walk through their maze one time. There are six teams and three mazes. They're all the same but there are three sets of judges to send three teams through at once so everything doesn't take five hundred years.

Our maze is confusing. I feel like we've been shrunk down to the size of ants and shoved into a crazy straw. The whole time Donna, Brooke, Reed and me are walking through it, all I can think of is how I have the easy part. They're the ones who have to guide me. But it's not until I put the earplugs in, after the cables attach me to Reed, that I start to realize how hard what I have to do might turn out to be.

We're in the hall practicing with me at the end of the cables for the very first time. All of us are wearing outfits of magicians, with capes going all the way to the floor and matching red bow ties. The cape they ordered for Cameron actually fits me pretty good but I'm so nervous I feel like I might spew the organic quinoa with raisins Brooke's mom made us this morning for breakfast all over it.

Okay, do not think about that.

Once Mrs. A. tightens the blindfold over my eyes, the

first pluck to the center cable comes. It doesn't tickle like Cameron's laughs made me think it would. It's just this huge *brooooong* all around the middle part of me that won't quit. Kind of annoying.

I swallow and lick my lips then move one foot forward. I can feel my heart. The buzz from the center cable spreads out to my arms and fingers and my foot can't remember how to take the next step. I'm scared. I can't see anything and all I can hear is my heart beating faster and faster. Everything's dark and all I have to connect me to the world is this annoying buzz that's making me feel the fillings in my teeth.

Why did I agree to do this? *Why* did Cameron have to catch the flu one night before the competition? I want to stop feeling like I'm lost in space. I want to rip these stupid earplugs out to hear the noise of the hall and check to see if there are strangers passing by and feeling sorry for the statue who's forgotten how to use her feet.

Someone comes up to me. Whoever it is grabs my wrist, but not in a bossy way. Now, they're squeezing my elbow.

I know who it is. I just do. I feel him put something on my head and know it's my blue fedora.

I slide a finger under the blindfold, careful not to rub the shrimp off my cheek. When I do, I see the backs of Meowsie's sneakers walking away from me down the hall.

There is no try.

The pluck to the center cable comes. I know exactly what I have to do so I take one step and then another.

I don't believe it.

I think I might be tilting just like Cameron! I sign KYLE CONSTANTINI in the air with big letters — who cares what I look like? I need the letters to be big so that I can feel big — so I can tell which way I'm tilting.

It's the left. I wonder why Cameron kept going right and I go left. I wonder what it is about not being able to hear or see that would make you not be able to walk in a straight line. I mean, all you have to do is put one foot in front of the other. Why do we need our eyes and ears to do that? Who knew it could turn you in circles just to *move*?

The buzz in the center cable stops completely so I do, too. The first tap comes. It's on the side I'm tilting toward so I turn to that side.

Weird.

All of a sudden, I wish there was a way for someone to send me the message that I'd made the turn okay. I can't believe none of us thought about that before. I wonder if Cameron wanted it, too, but he just didn't ask. It's amazing how much of me needs to know I did all right.

The pluck to the center cable comes again so I just start advancing. I think it says a lot when you choose to move even when you're not sure you'll get where you're headed. We make four or five turns—I kinda lose count—and then someone is tapping my shoulder. I slide the blindfold off and pull out the plugs.

"That's all we have time for," Mrs. A. tells me.

What? Is she kidding me? I need more practice! This wasn't enough! And now it's time to go *into the maze*?

"Mrs. Arceneau." I grab her arm.

She looks at me through her rose-colored glasses.

"This isn't easy what you're doing, Kyle," she says. "But maybe you and this moment were meant for each other."

A moment and a breakthrough.

For a second, I can almost hear a choir—like from the Circle of Life. I try to move toward the door of the arena but kind of can't. Then I can. Sometimes you think there's no way you can do something but then all of a sudden you just do.

We pass through the entrance. While the judges are watching the school before us—they're just rolling their team member on a dolly dressed like a spaceship so I know we can cream them—we decide to reach out to Cameron.

Brooke's mom draws the most perfect little orange shrimp on Reed's cheek and fills it in. It looks good on him. He, me, Donna and Brooke get together for a group selfie—a grelfie—on Donna's phone. I'm standing between Reed and Brooke with Donna on the other side of Brooke holding the phone out in front of us. We squeeze together and I feel Reed's arm around my shoulders, fingers curling at my neck. I lift both arms to put one around Reed and one around Brooke while Donna yells, "Say provolone!"

The four of us break apart and we text the pic to Cameron so he can see how much we're thinking of him right at the moment we go into the maze. Then Donna says, "Okay, lemme get a shot of just Reed and Kyle." She lifts her phone again. "Since they're the ones that are gonna be attached in the maze. We can get a before and an after."

Reed and I shoot a look at each other and he shrugs with kind of an upside-down smile like, why not?

Why not.

We scoot in together again until our capes almost blend into one. We're so close, I think I can pick out the soap he used this morning. He smells like fresh limes. I feel starry and light as I smile into the camera on Donna's phone and that's the second I spot Sheroo.

Her eyes meet mine and I feel my smile shrink as she shakes her head at me with that disappointed look of hers. Then she turns on one heel and walks straight back out one of the doors.

"All good?" Reed asks me.

I swallow once, twice. A prickly feeling spreads under my arms. Like the kind you feel when someone brakes in the car, really fast and unexpected. It's like your body is trying to calm down after barely escaping an accident. Only I don't feel like I've escaped. I feel like I'm about to go straight into traffic and have no idea how to drive.

"I think so." My voice comes out wobbly. For a second, the arena starts to spin.

"Hey." Reed touches my wrist with the tippiest tips of his fingers. "Kyle."

I focus on his bow tie.

"You're not doing this by yourself, you know."

I look him in the eye.

"Trust."

The earplugs go in. The blindfold slides on and erases Reed's familiar face from view. The world goes silent, and dark.

The maze is long.

A lot longer than it seemed when I walked through it before. At first, I get that hot, panicky feeling in my throat—like I just want to see and hear again *right now*—but I take really long, slow, deep breaths and think about how it's my friends I'm connected to, and how these ones aren't gonna let me fall.

As I take steps in—I hope—a straight line with the

buzz running around my waist, I realize the one thing that was not in our plan is some kind of sign to let me know when I've made the right step, and when I've made the wrong. I think about what it must be like to be a wayfinder on a cloudy night when they can't see any stars. They know the stars are there. Stars don't ever go away. Just the ability to see them sometimes does. So I guess that's what wayfinders learn how to do. They search out the truths that are already hanging out in their houses of power, and choose to point themselves in the right direction.

I try not to worry that I might be tilting. I just keep taking these big, slow breaths until not being able to see or hear starts to feel a little more normal. The buzz stops and, automatically, my feet freeze. I wait for the tap to come and it does. I turn in its direction and the cable goes *crazy*! I don't get what that means!

I can't tell if the side cable has been plucked or tapped or dropped but the message has *really* stopped making sense. So I just stand there—imagining myself out at sea when the sky has swallowed the light—and wait for a signal to get clear. This is what we were missing. Signals to tell us how to correct our course.

There's scrambling around and the cables go tight again. I can feel Reed at the other end of them and get very still. All I can do is wait until I understand what my stars are trying to tell me—right now, in this very

215

moment. The cables go a little loose and I feel movement. Then they tighten again. A solid tap comes on one side and I think, *Brooke!* I know her energy. I take a small step in that direction and the cables tighten. And somehow the feel of those cables gives me the confidence I need to turn all the way.

A powerful pluck comes to the middle cable and I start walking. I think about Reed, and how we've already made so many circles of infinity, and I know in my heart that being able to make out the stars in another person is not just important during combat. It's probably more important when you depend on each other and are on the same team. And all of a sudden it hits me.

Some moments, we can actually sense—not through our eyes and ears, but through the stars in the houses of our power—that there's this strong, true thing, always waiting to flow into us. So the next time the cable does something I don't totally understand, I get still. Because I trust that the power at the other end will sooner or later tell me whatever I need to know. If I can just be patient enough to listen to the part of it that already speaks inside of me.

The end of the maze comes. By the time we all make it out together, I'm actually sweating! Brooke slides my blindfold off and is smiling at me as Reed and Donna high-five. I fish out the earplugs and hear Marcy and even Meowsie cheering from their seats, which are close to the exit of our maze. I'm so happy to see and hear again! But another, more quieter part of me looks straight at Marcy, remembering how sometimes she takes out her hearing aids so she can feel the special power of the mystery. I'm relieved to be out of the maze but at the same time, it's weird. Because if I had the chance, I think I'd actually do it all again. Like somehow there's more treasure in there, if I'm not too chicken in the face of the great unknown to go back in after it.

"You were *this* close to hitting a wall!" Brooke tells me.

"Really?" I laugh.

She nods with a laugh, too. "I can't believe we never came up with a signal to say, 'No! Wrong way!'"

"That's just what I was thinking when I was in there!" I tell her.

"After that, I tried my best to just, I don't know," she says. "Communicate with you to stop—and you did. I couldn't let you hit that wall."

I laugh and she bear hugs me. As I sink with relief into her hug, the sounds in the arena overwhelm me. I can't believe I never noticed before. How we're always swimming in this confetti roar and don't even realize it's there. Brooke and me let go as a scratchy voice comes on over the speakers. There's a lady with a microphone on the big, foamy platform set up in the middle of all the mazes. I imagine they look like enormous circuit boards, tossed all over the floor.

"Well done, teams. You've done an excellent job representing your middle schools and you should be proud."

Brooke, Reed, Donna and me all clap and kinda put our arms around each other in a line as we wait to hear what comes next.

"Now, we need you all to be in attendance at the awards ceremony when the winners will be announced, after the judges have had an opportunity to evaluate your performances and tally up your scores."

People are shushing everybody all over the floor and the lady smiles.

"So, again, well done. And we'll see you tomorrow evening."

As we're all getting to our cars outside, I search the parking lot for some sign of Sheroo. Though the bigger part of me knows there's not really a chance she'll still be here.

I let out a huge sigh and feel a tug on my cape. I turn around and see Reed.

"You were great in there," he tells me. "I was worried about you at the first, but you were really, really great in there."

He squints at the tip of my fedora in the sun, and that's the moment I finally let myself accept how I really feel about him.

"*We* were really, really great in there." I smile at him. "English Boy."

Chapter Fifteen

That night is the Georgia O'Keeffe Harvest Carnival and, just like they promised, Mom and Dad get Uncle Jack to take me and Meowsie.

"Hey. Let's go to the thing at your school and then we can come home and watch the old *Clash of the Titans*," Meowsie tells me as I'm in the bathroom getting ready.

I tip my head in the mirror and smack my blue lips. "You just want to see Andromeda's bahameda as she comes out of the bath."

"Kyle."

I wanted to make my own costume this year, just like Mom, only I can't sew dragon heads or whatever so mine's a little more easy. I needed to wear my fedora so the whole rest of my idea came from that. With a classic white tee, I have on blue jean shorts, striped blue tights, blue suspenders, skinny blue tie, blue lipstick and, of course, my blue fedora. I thought about making my whole face blue but then decided I didn't want all that paint on me. Instead, I just got some blue glitter to go around my eyes. Looks pretty kick so I think I made the right choice.

"What are you supposed to be anyway?" Meows asks me. "You look kind of … aqua."

"What are you?" I ask him.

His outfit is pretty normal. The only thing sort of different is that he has a goatee painted on.

"I'm Mr. Arriéta."

"Really?" I turn from the Meows in the mirror to the real Meows standing behind me. "That's pretty cool. You look good as Mr. Arriéta."

He tugs at his shirt. "Well, what are you?"

I dab just a little more glitter by one of my eyes to even them out and turn my head to inspect my work just like Mom inspected hers. Then I stand up straight and look at the only face I have.

"I'm a defender of the Blue Fedora Code."

Soon as we get to the carnival, Meowsie and Marcy find each other like magnets. They come up with a strategy to have the best chance on the cakewalk and Meowsie starts to sink the entire ten bucks Uncle Jack gave each of us before we left the house at that booth.

I wanna scope out my options. As I look around, I have to admit I'm pretty curious to know what Reed'll come dressed as. Maybe something from *Wolverine*? Or, ooh! Something British. Like a guard in front of Buckingham Palace or the guy from David Beckham.

Brooke makes her way through the crowd to me with a sneaky grin on her whiskered face. She's dressed up as a black cat—which isn't the most original idea in the Milky Way but she looks cute. From the way she's twirling her tail, I'm pretty sure she knows how cute she looks, too.

"What are you supposed to be?" she asks me.

I'm not in the right mood to go into the whole Blue Fedora Code right at the moment so instead of answering I ask her if she's seen Sheroo.

"Yep." She nods. "She and Smiley are at the fishing booth. Smiley's so sweet. Dressed up as a cotton-tailed rabbit."

Smiley is Sheroo's baby half sister. Her real name is Melissa but everyone calls her Smiley.

"Have you seen anyone from NAVS?" I ask. "Cameron or Donna—"

"No, I haven't seen Reed." She looks at me with those sharp, smart eyes of hers. "And Cameron's still out of commission," she adds. "Think he will be for at least a week. But Donna's hanging out somewhere. She came dressed as—"

"Don't tell me. A dolphin."

"Surprisingly, no." Brooke nods over at the space between the cakewalk and the ring toss. I turn to look and see Donna signing something at Marcy, who came as a sunflower. She laughs at whatever Donna just told her.

Donna's costume takes me completely by surprise. She's pretty striking with her red hair pulled back and a crown of violets around her brow. She's dressed as a medieval maiden.

Brooke and I look around at the rest of the booths. For most of them — except the cakewalk and the eighth-grade dunk — you collect tickets that you can exchange for prizes at the end of the night. I spot the prize counter and see that one of the things you can pick are stickers of bats. Scratch 'n' sniff!

"What do you think bats smell like?" I ask Brooke.

She shrugs. "Guano, maybe? Cavern."

"What does cavern smell like?"

"Guano?"

Thank you, Brookipedia.

I move up to the counter and ask the parent volunteer what the bat stickers smell like.

"Licorice," she says. "They're one of the most popular prizes tonight. That and the spooky caramel apples from Yankee Doodle Candy. Everybody waits all year for those."

Brooke taps me on the shoulder and I turn around. From across the room, Sheroo is staring the both of us down. She's not with Sasha or Mercedes or any of her other new friends. She's just standing a few yards from the fishing booth dressed like a flapper. Her costume is so great. She looks incredibly cool with a big feather sticking out of her headband, a super-long pearly necklace tied in a knot and a dress with strings that swish like crazy every time she moves.

I feel that familiar crunch between my ribs. Last year, it was so much fun when the three of us hung out. Brooke was the smart one, Sheroo was the crazy one and I was— what was I? It's hard to know which one *you* are when you're with your friends. But anyway we were the perfect trio. We drew SKB in bubble letters on all of our binders with metallic paint pens, and Sheroo even carved our initials onto a table in the library this one time when she was supposed to be reading a book about some war but was bored. She didn't get in trouble, though. I guess Mrs. Cromeans didn't make the connection.

"Incoming," Brooke says. Then she snaps the piece of Dubble Bubble she's been chewing. It's Halloween, *the* candy event of the year, and as Sheroo walks up to us my stomach's so tight I can't even think about enjoying all the sugar.

"Hey," she says.

223

"Hey," I echo.

"Hey."

Brooke rolls one of her hands to keep the convo moving along. She looks at Sheroo, then me.

"You guys do realize how ridiculous you're being," Brooke says, after Sheroo and I have been having a staring contest, practically.

"You're not helping," Sheroo tells Brooke.

"Well, what will help?" Brooke asks. "Cloning Reed?"

My face goes hot and I look around to make sure nobody heard what Brooke just frisbeed out there.

"I mean, let's face it, people can't exactly control who they have crushes on."

"Brooke," I say through my teeth.

"What? It's the truth. You guys should just put all this behind you and be friends again," she goes on. "It's not like the two of you are the only ones this stupid argument has affected."

We both look at Brooke.

"Who else?" Sheroo asks.

"Hello?" Brooke flips her tail. "You think I like seeing my two best friends in the world split up over a *guy*?"

"Well, this isn't really about a guy anymore. Is it?" Sheroo says.

I am totally and completely stumped. And alarmed.

"Look, the point is, if you were in love with Reed all

along," she tells me, "you should have just *said* so from the start."

In love with Reed? All along? Saying so *out loud*?

"This isn't about Reed," Sheroo goes on, and I want to beg her to keep it down.

"This isn't?" Brooke asks.

"Okay, maybe it is, kind of," Sheroo concedes. "But it's about more than that and Kyle knows it!"

"I am not having this conversation right now," I say. Because, first of all, I kind of have no idea what she's talking about and it's scaring me. What else could this be about except her crush on Reed? But, second of all, hello? Having a big, ol' heart-to-heart about all this super private stuff way out in the open in the middle of the carnival? We might as well be on a sunken stage in the Civic Center.

"Well, when *will* you have it?" Sheroo demands.

I stare at her, then look at Brooke, then back at Sheroo.

"Just—" I shake my head and drop both hands, turning on one heel to make my way to the doors of the auditorium. I push out into the cool night air. Sheroo is hard on my heels but, out of the corner of my eye, I can see Brooke has turned her back and stayed inside.

"So, it's *true*, then?" Sheroo trails me down the steps. I go to the sidewalk and turn the corner toward the outdoor basketball courts. "Why can't you just admit it?"

"Sheroo, you're embarrassing me."

"Look, will you just quit walking?" she tells me.

"No."

She follows me all the way to the sidewalks by the gym. There's still a lot of construction going on and I wonder when the heck they're gonna finish.

"Perfect," I mutter.

"Finally!" she huffs after I stop, the strings on her dress swishing back and forth like spaghetti car-wash sponges.

But I don't stop for her. I stop because, of all people, Ino Nevarez is sitting on the rock wall near the gym—by himself. He's not even wearing a costume. I blow out a long breath and wonder how all of a sudden this night got so Count Crapula.

"Kyle, all you have to do," Sheroo says, "is be honest with me. Look, I'm sorry I got mad at you at the beginning of the year over that note for the NAVS meeting. That was"—she takes a breath and lets it out—"just stupid of me. But it was also stupid of *you* not to be honest with *me* and just admit that you like him, too."

"Sheroo, where are you going?" Sheroo's baby sister Smiley pops out behind us. "Mom said we're a'posed to stay together," she says in her tiny voice. I turn to look at her in her bunny costume. She looks cute enough to squish. Her little nose looks just like a mini strawberry.

"Go back inside, Smi," Sheroo says. "I'll be right there."

"No."

"Smiley, just *gim*me a minute!"

"But Mom said!"

"Well, go *find* Mom!" Sheroo yells.

But Smiley ignores her. Instead, she climbs over the orange tape surrounding the bar with the basketball hoop attached to the backboard. It's been yanked out of the asphalt, base carved straight out of the ground. It's standing but it doesn't look super stable.

"Smiley," I start, "I wouldn't—"

The sound of her scream splits the air like a piccolo being snapped.

"Smiley!" Sheroo kicks off her heels and kneels by her sister. "She's stuck!"

Smiley makes a funny sound as the long bar attached to the backboard has now tumbled completely and has pinned her little chest to the ground.

"Get it up!" I yell.

I try to lift it off Smiley but there is just no way.

"Sheroo, run!" I say. "Go get help! I don't think she can breathe properly!"

"Oh, my God!"

"Sheroo, please, just get a hold of yourself! She'll be okay if we help her."

Smiley makes another strange sound, her face getting as pink as her nose as she flails her hands. I had no idea these backboards were so heavy!

I try again to shove the bar off Smiley's chest. Sheroo is just sitting there, flailing her own arms and crying her sister's name. The bar barely budges. I need help. Fast. I'm shaking as I try to get my shoulder under the bar when all of a sudden it starts to come up. It's working!

"Pull her out!"

It's a guy's voice, like a roar. I look over my shoulder and see that Ino has forced the bar up just enough so that Smiley can wriggle free.

"Pull her out!" he growls again, his face purple.

I gather Smiley's legs and swing her out from under the bar, which Ino drops with a horrible clang. He slumps on the ground and takes a heavy breath.

"Smiley!" Sheroo tries to grab her but I stop her.

"No, don't move her more yet! Smiley, can you hear me?" I ask.

Smiley starts to whimper.

"Can you move your arms by yourself?" I ask. She moves a few of her little fingers.

"Girls, what—" Mrs. Malagares is standing on the other side of the rock wall. "What are you doing out here? Why did you leave the carnival?"

"I'm sorry," Sheroo sobs.

"What in God's name—?"

Mrs. Malagares scurries to Smiley, who's still huddled near my lap.

"What happened? Melissa!"

She scoops up her youngest daughter and turns on her oldest.

"Are you insane? You were supposed to be looking out for your sister, not—" She casts a glance at Ino, still catching his breath. "Get inside. Now!"

Sheroo scrambles to her feet and grabs her shoes, making a sprint for the sidewalk.

"Kyle, you too!" she shouts at me.

"Yes, Mrs. Malagares."

But then she ignores me as she carries a whimpering Smiley behind Sheroo and just keeps bawling her out.

I'm shaking. I'm shaking and my hands are Popsicles. Smiley would have been crushed if that bar had fallen on her harder. She wasn't breathing right. I don't know how long she would have lasted. I look over at Ino and think he might be shaking, too.

"You okay?" I ask him.

He looks at me with clear green eyes.

"Thank you," I tell him, still so shocked I can hardly believe we're having this conversation. "There's no way I could have helped her by myself."

He pushes himself up and wipes his palms on his pants.

"All gravy, Wonder Woman."

Then he climbs the steps in the opposite direction of

the carnival and disappears toward the dark entrance to the gym.

★　★　★

Brooke rushes me the minute I'm in the door.

"What happened?"

I just look at her and swallow. She pulls me by the tie toward a booth in the corner.

"Sheroo's family left! Mrs. Malagares was talking all mad to Principal Bracamontes and then she dragged Sheroo and Smiley to the car and just took off!"

I tell Brooke what happened and watch as her eyes bug out.

"Do you think Mrs. Malagares is taking Smiley to the hospital to get X-rays?"

"I might, if I was her."

"I hope she's okay." Brooke wrings her hands. I hardly ever see her get this emotional.

She starts to calm down, though, as we do the bean-bag toss—which is easy but at least you're guaranteed tickets that way—and the suction darts—which are a little harder to hit the bull's-eye, but I still try. I miss, but still score a ticket for landing inside one of the inner circles.

At the end of the hour, I don't have a ton of tickets to

my name but Uncle Jack says, "Five more minutes," so Brooke and I go to the counter to claim our prizes.

Brooke picks out a pair of wax lips and a laser gun key chain.

"At least you'll get a new bat sticker," Brooke tells me as she points her teeny laser at me and fires. She's one of the only people—besides Meowsie—who knows about my collection.

"What'll it be, blue girl?" the volunteer asks behind the counter.

I hand over all of my tickets and make my selection.

"With sprinkles, please."

★   ★   ★

"Can we make just one quick stop?" I ask Uncle Jack on the way home.

He looks at the clock on his dash and says, "Has to be quick if you guys still want to stay up to watch *Clash of the Titans*."

"I promise it'll be very, very fast."

He palms the steering wheel. "Where to?"

I give him the address I've seen every single day from the bus, guts curling up tighter than Brooke's ringlets after a storm.

I've always wondered what the inside of a town house

is like. Uncle Jack has to get a special visitor pass on his white Corvette at the gate to go inside. There's a fountain with a light shining up that turns the water blue and aqua and green and then blue again. I never get to see that during the day. But all of the trees and the bushes look cut clean and straight, just like they always do, as we drive up to the number I memorized by heart the day I first looked it up in the directory.

"This one," I say, breathless. I swallow and try to suck in more air but can barely get enough. The inside of my cheeks are dry as Texas.

Uncle Jack puts the car in park but leaves it running. As I pop out, Meowsie shoots me a funny look.

IT'S ALL UNDER CONTROL. I JUST NEED TO DO THIS.

I've thought about what this would be like so many times I can't believe it's actually happening. Feels like a dream.

I climb up the steps to the second floor and go straight to unit 2515. I take like three or four long breaths to get my heart to stop beating so hard before I finally work up the courage to press a thumb to the skinny doorbell. I hear it ring on the inside and then footsteps.

I squeeze my eyes shut and cross my fingers, knees and toes that he answers.

"Fedora?"

I open my eyes and see that Reed has opened the door.

He looks as surprised as I feel nervous. He's not wearing a costume, just a navy-blue tee and some old plaid shorts and bare feet.

"What are you doing here?"

I quickly uncross my knees as he grabs some old, chewed-up loafers from inside the hall closet and slips them on before stepping outside and clicking his front door shut.

"You didn't come to the carnival."

He glances over his shoulder. "Yeah, it's"—he takes a quick breath—"complicated."

I look at the closed door and feel my heart wish that I could make all the complicated stuff behind it easier for Reed somehow.

"Did you get any trick-or-treaters?" I ask.

"Not until you." He smiles. "David told me to just turn out the lights but I thought that might be a bit rude. Even though we don't have any sweets to hand out."

"That's okay," I say, "because I brought you this." I pull from its waxy sack the caramel apple from Yankee Doodle Candy. "Used all my tickets for it."

His eyes get all shiny and soft. "You didn't have to do that," he says quietly.

"Yeah, well." I shrug. "You know."

"Thank you, Kyle."

He accepts my gift. Then we stare at each other like a

couple of speechless dorf nuggets for about ten seconds. That doesn't seem like a long time but, really, it depends on what you're doing.

"You're welcome," I finally answer.

Then I lean in—com*pletel*y without thinking—and peck his cheek. When I pull away, there's a pair of blue lips on his skin where the shrimp used to be. And when I see them there, I know for certain the next thing I need to do.

"Well, I gotta go." I motion to the stairs. "My brother and uncle are waiting for me."

He nods but doesn't say anything. Just stares at me, dumbstruck.

I hurry toward the steps when I hear him call.

"Fedora!"

I stop and turn around.

"I owe you," he tells me. Then he lifts the caramel apple and gives me the most lopsided smile in the history of smiling.

"No worries, sport," I say. "We're even." Then I give him my trademark click and wink before running down to the first floor and hopping into my uncle's idling car.

That night in my room, after I wash all the blue out of my hair and off my eyes and my lips, I see Mom has laid out my clean gym clothes on the end of the bed. Before I put on my Dear-Pluto-you'll-always-be-a-planet-in-my-heart sleep tee, I slip into the shorts and shirt and stand on the edge of the tub in the bathroom with my hair all wet to look in the mirror over the sink—just to make sure I'm not imagining things.

Maybe this last time Mom stuck them in the dryer they shrunk. Or maybe sometime between punching Ino in the gut and joining forces with him to save Smiley, I grew. Whatever the case, my uniform fits.

I study my scrubbed face in the mirror and think about how Sheroo told me I should have just been honest with her from the start. But I know now, after everything, that the person I *really* needed to be honest with from the very beginning was me. Then I would have been able to shoot it straight with her about Reed and with my mom about NAVS in the first place. It's crazy how hard that can be to do sometimes. But I guess when you're getting mixed signals from everything outside you, you just have to dig a little deeper until you reach the door to the house of your own power.

And maybe that's what people mean when they say you have to find a way to be comfortable in your *own* skin.

Chapter Sixteen

The next morning, there's just one important phone call I need to make before the awards ceremony. It's nowhere near 7:07, but I dial the number I haven't dialed in more than a month but will know till my dying breath.

"Hello?" Sheroo answers.

"It's me," I say.

"I know."

Silence. Then: "Did you stay late at the carnival?"

I switch my mom's phone from one ear to the other.

"Not really," I say.

"Did you and Brooke hang out?"

"Yeah." I take a breath. "Is Smiley okay?"

"She's doing a lot better," Sheroo tells me. "Just a little scared but she got over it. Thank God that other big guy was there."

"Yeah. Thank God."

Never thought I'd hear myself agree with *that*.

"Saw you getting ready to go onstage at the Civic Center," she says. "Guess you weren't being completely dishonest about NAVS."

"No," I say. "Not with you, anyway."

"Brooke told me you had to wear a blindfold and a pair of earplugs. Was it weird?"

"Very," I admit. "But also interesting. In a way."

I want to ask her why she didn't stay to watch but I know why.

"Sheroo, I'm sorry," I say. "About everything. I know how much Reed means to you and I really don't want it to mess up our friendship anymore." My face is on fire. "But you're right," I go on. "I do kind of like him. I have kind of liked him for a while now."

Quiet, then: "Well, does he like you back?"

"I have" — I swallow — "no idea. All I can tell you is how I feel about him. I like to keep those kinds of things, you know, crushes and everything, to myself because it's a little embarrassing."

"Why embarrassing?"

"I don't know." I lick my lips. "I guess I'm just kind of private about things like that." I take another breath. "But, in this situation, my friendship with you is more important than my scared feelings about being honest. So..."

"I've really missed you," she fills in the gap — and

relief washes over me like a spout under the curly slides at Wet 'N Wild Waterworld.

"I've missed you, too!" I practically shout. It feels *so* good to say it! "Nothing is the same without you, Sheroo. As much as I've loved making new friends this year, there's no one that can take the place of you."

I imagine her on the other end of the line, thinking about what I just said.

"I love the cat," she starts slowly. "He's so stinkin' round."

"You mean Len?" I smile. "He's a friendship cat. The purple is for friendship."

"Leave it to you to know that."

"What do you mean?"

"I mean that you're in things like NAVS and suddenly you're all super smart girl."

I smile even bigger. All I need now are my baby blue glasses!

I close my eyes and take a breath to work up the guts to say what I called to ask in the first place.

"Sheroo, do you want to come with me to the awards ceremony tonight?"

I wouldn't hold it against her if she said she'd rather not. Because maybe the whole Reed fiasco is just too painful and fresh and just—weird. You never know, sometimes. The heart is a mysterious vessel. But then her answer comes shining through.

"What time should I be ready?"

Mom got me a new shirt for the awards ceremony and I don't like it. It's too shirty—the buttons are *gold*, for crying out loud—but I wear it anyway.

On our way to pick up Sheroo before we go to the Civic Center, I write my name in the window of Dad's Denali with a magic wand. Well, I mean, I write it with my finger but I draw a wand next to it. The weather is dark and rainy so the windows are nice and foggy for drawing. After I do my name and the wand, I draw Circe. Except I run out of room for her tail so I have to draw it straight up against the side. She looks alarmed.

When we get there, all the teams are with their families and friends and I start to feel really excited. Even though it's black and stormy outside, in the arena there's lights and commotion and we all get special name tags with our school on them. I pin mine on and look at Mom, feeling proud.

Cameron's still down with the flu but Donna, Brooke, Reed and me all sit in a row together with Sheroo, Meowsie and Marcy and all the grown-ups behind us. The team that carted their blindfolded member through the maze on a space dolly is sitting to one side of us and I all of a sudden get this really weird feeling.

If they win, we lose. If we win, they lose.

You see people in movies and things or read about them in books and it's always about them winning against the other guys. But what about the other guys? If you look at the story from their side, who are the other guys to them?

It's a little bit like me and Sheroo. We can't both have Reed. I mean, not in that way. Have I been the other guy to her this whole time? I think about Principal Bracamontes saying we're not all here to take justice into our own hands and wonder: Can the stars in the house of our power show us another way?

"Welcome, students, to the seventh-annual NAVS awards ceremony. Tonight, we will be announcing which team will represent our city at the regional competition in Phoenix, Arizona, for a chance to go to Nationals. Six fantastic teams have pitted their very best efforts against our mazes and they should all be commended."

The lady on the stage starts to clap and everyone else does, too. I glance at Donna and notice the look on her face. Which is kinda like, *Enough with the chitchat, Wanda Wellwish. Let's get on with it, already.*

"Tonight, three teams have earned their honorable mentions."

Oh, great flying, lipless llamas. Please don't let us have an honorable mention.

"And the honorable mentions, in no particular order, go to—" The lady shuffles some papers on the podium and I start to chew the top of the nail right off my thumb. It even bleeds a little at the cuticle. Nast.

She names three schools that are *not* Georgia O'Keeffe. I lick my lips and Reed catches my eye. He gives me this super-little nod and I do it back. At the very least, we'll get third. But I don't want to get third. And I can tell Reed doesn't want third any more than me and Donna. We wanna go to Phoenix and whoop the butts off the mazes they have there.

"In third place," the lady says. "Santa Rosa Middle School from the Northeast Heights."

I'm going to pee in my pants.

I'm eleven years old in sixth grade and I'm gonna pee my pants like a baby. I *hate* suspense!

Brooke grabs my hand and squeezes it on one side and Sheroo takes the other.

"In second place—"

Please say the name of the other school. Oh, please, God, please, let us go to Phoenix for Regionals. I'll never ask for anything until Christmas if you just let us go to Phoenix for Regionals. I'll keep on not punching people and guard the Blue Fedora Code and not even *think* about smearing anything of Roger's with toe jam, no matter how much he stinks up the car like Right Guard.

"—Georgia O'Keeffe Middle School."

A cheer goes up.

Only it's not from our part of the arena. The cheering team is the one that wasn't called. The team that knows since we got second, they got first. I turn to Brooke and she looks like she's gonna cry. And Donna actually *is* crying a little! And when I see that, I feel a big tear plop on the shirty shirt Mom bought me and, right then and there, I realize one thing about not winning.

Losing sucks.

★ ★ ★

Michael_C: You there?

the_amazing_kyle: You know I am.

Michael_C: I'm nervous.

the_amazing_kyle: I figured

Michael_C: About the concert.

the_amazing_kyle: yeah I know. But don't worry.
the nervousness goes away.

Michael_C: When?

the_amazing_kyle: like in a year

the_amazing_kyle: j/k

Michael_C: Your team was really good at the competition.

I swallow back a salty wad. It's like a tiny water balloon, filled up with tears.

Michael_C: I'm sorry you guys didn't get first.
the_amazing_kyle: It's ok
Michael_C: You were still truly a-maze-ing.

I smile with half my face. The other half is still too
down in the dumps to budge.

the_amazing_kyle: thx

The truth is, I still don't totally feel like talking about it.

Michael_C: You probably don't want to talk about it
right now. But I just wanted to encourage you.
Winning isn't everything.

I look at the ceiling. There's a flag on Mars up there
but I can't tell from what country.

the_amazing_kyle: yeah but it's not nothing.

Meowsie doesn't type anything for a while. I imagine
him roaming his eyes over the carpet of his room. I think
about how when you're on Instant, you don't get to see

243

everything about how the other person is reacting. Then I think about how, even in real lives when a person is right in front of you, you still sometimes don't catch everything that's happening inside them. I mean, look at Ino, for paunch's sake. Even *he* ended up having more than just a couple of turd alarms inside waiting to bust out and save the day.

Michael_C: Losing can be the secret win.

I take a deep breath and then let it out in a sigh.

Michael_C: It's when you lose that you gain something other than winning, but it's a hidden kind of winning. So you have to know where to look for it.
the_amazing_kyle: Meows what are you talking about
Michael_C: I'm talking about the chance that losing gives you. To figure out where and how you really want to spend the strength you still have for the next battle.

Spending strength in the battle? He sounds one Lucky Charm shy of a complete breakfast. But then I remember everything Coach has been teaching us, and how maybe it's the mistakes we make that end up giving us the best chances to enter the house of our power and correct our course. I wonder if Meows heard all this stuff at *his* school.

the_amazing_kyle: Is that from Mr Arrieta or something??

Michael_C: Not Mr. Arriéta.

the_amazing_kyle: well who then

I wait for a second as my brother picks out his answer from the psychotronic layers of the Meowsiesphere.

Michael_C: It's something Marcy has helped me to see.

It snows on the day of Meowsie's concert. Just a skinny coat that looks like powdered sugar on a waffle as big as the city. I invite Marcy to go with me because I know Meowsie will appreciate that and because I hope Marcy will, too.

The flakes are coming down all soft as she and me and Roger and Mom and Dad walk into the bank. It's already decorated with dreidels and Christmas trees even though Thanksgiving hasn't even gotten here yet. There's this fat snake of gold tinsel wrapping around the curving staircase inside the bank and that's where Meowsie and his voices of the future are gonna sing.

I haven't heard Meowsie practice. Not even once. He won't let anyone hear him. I'm not sure where he practices or if he soundproofs his bedroom or what but when I see him and his singing friends line up on the stairs, I get nervous *for* him. So at least that way, maybe he can just concentrate on the song.

Dad shakes hands with Mr. Arriéta. Even though I haven't met him, I know exactly who he is. Everyone sits down in the audience and a lady I don't recognize raises a conducting wand to get Meowsie and the rest of the singers to start. It's super quiet at first, just voices. And the first thing that comes to my head is that if this is what the future sounds like, I wouldn't mind at all.

There's a bee in my chest. Not as strong as the one that I got from the cables but I can still feel it. I imagine a cable attaching me to Meowsie and every time he opens his mouth I feel it ring. I look at Roger. For once, he doesn't have his face plastered to his phone. He's just looking at Meowsie. The song is kind of sad and happy at the same time, like something you wish you could play in your bedroom at night when the ceiling is full of too many pictures and you can't get to sleep.

I sneak a look at Marcy and see that her eyes are all filled up with water—like a great, buttery tear might just *blop* on her shoulder if she even thinks about blinking.

I know just how she feels.

Once the song is over, the whole bank is really quiet

even though it's filled with people. Someone moves a chair and it makes kind of a trumpet sound even though we're all sitting on carpet. And right in the space between the first song and the next, Marcy leans close to me and whispers with her sweet, yawny voice in my ear.

"Now *that* was worth fighting for."

★　★　★

Name: Kyle Alexandra Constantini
Age: 11 (+ 3 mos. + whatever many days)
School: Georgia O'Keeffe Middle
Purpose of Inventory: to state the bylaws and trilaws of the BLUE FEDORA CODE

I. As a founder, upholder and defender of the BLUE FEDORA CODE, I pledge to tell myself the truth and, as best as I can, not hide <u>from myself</u> what I am really thinking and feeling.

II. As a founder, upholder and defender of the BLUE FEDORA CODE, I pledge to find ways to tell other people (for example Mom, Sheroo, Brooke, Meowsie, Marcy, Reed, etc. (but maybe not Roger)) the truth about what all I am

really thinking and feeling (and doing—
especially if I'm grounded or otherwise in
trubbs) soon as I figure out what that is.

III. As a founder, upholder and defender of the
BLUE FEDORA CODE, I pledge to give other people a
chance to figure out the truth of who they are
(or hope to be) and to watch for the guides
that are starting to shine under their skin.

IV. As a founder, upholder and defender of the
BLUE FEDORA CODE, I pledge to serve as the
captain of my heart; to look up into the night
sky of life when the seas are ferocious and
super bumpy (or even just enormous) and use
everything I've learned from my mistakes to
tap into the stars I know are always there.

Because I believe, by the strength of the truth
and the way of the wise, that we all have
constellations in our houses of power, just
waiting to rise.

(Hey, that rhymes.)

Acknowledgments

My thanks and total devotion, first and foremost, to the two most radiant points in my galaxy: my beloved husband, Shawn Gay, who daily improves the quality of my life by a magnitude of about five billion, and our beautiful daughter, Belinda, who really wanted a whale emoji by her name in the dedication.

My thanks, love and continued devotion to my excellent parents: Juan Salom, equal parts dad and cutman (bend your knees) and the perennially elegant Martha, of the 'Thank you, Master' salad (con el favor de Dios). To my role model and sister, Sandra Froehle, whose bubble comments on every manuscript I've written are, bar none, the raddest gift I have ever received—or will ever receive—in exchange for sharing my work. You rock my heart, güera musiquera. To my gorgeous baby sister, Sarah Moring, whose cotton-candy adoration of Kyle means the world to me. You *fill* my heart with your joy and implacable zeal for life, princess. To Captain John Salom, Jr. and Paul 'the Duke' Salom, the two most generous and supportive brothers in the Milky Way—no exaggeration. As loving, indivisible families go, se aventaron.

A huge thank you wrapped with a bow to Adrienne Allen Mirzayan, Lorena Hughes (Thank you, Elizabeth!!!!!!)

and Lynda 'Lynnie' R. Young, admired friends and loyal brain trust over the last decade. The three of you are brilliant, beautiful women without whose encouragement at pivotal moments my career as a novelist would have given up the ghost. Thanks, also, to the students of Radford School in 1999, 2000 and 2001; to Raul 'Bibi' Peláez; Steven R. Cranmer; Elizabeth 'Lizzie' Rose Stanton; Nicki 'Nick' Elson; E. T. Smith; Luanne 'Lu' Smith; Savannah Kuper; Kim Karras; Magdoline 'Mags' Asfahani; Southwest Writers of Albuquerque and Chelsea Gilmore.

This book would not be bound and on the shelves were it not for the faith of my agent, John M. Cusick—an unflagging champion and a master at providing context at the intersection of art and commerce—and Cheryl Klein, an incredibly dedicated, conscientious and hardworking editor. I lift up my cup to you both. My gratitude toward the two of you knows no bounds.

Gracias, del alma, a Toñio, Chole, Rafaél y Amelia, con orgullo y sonrisas sobre recuerdos de una juventud feliz, pero tambien con lagrimitas tiernas y abundantes. I miss you.

Finally, fedoras off to The Incredible Bulk, Sophia Loren, my fat girl and inspiration for every feline character I have ever written.

Blessings, without number, on each of your luminous heads.
And Sandra cried . . .

This book was edited by Cheryl Klein and designed by Mary Claire Cruz. The production was supervised by Elizabeth Krych and Rebekah Wallin. The text was set in Janson Mt Std, with display type set in Hand Scribble Sketch Rock. This book was printed and bound by R. R. Donnelley in Crawfordsville, Indiana. The manufacturing was supervised by Angelique Browne.